The Man wit

'I couldn't help thinki
Mum wouldn't even
suppose she'd got used to Dad running
get fed up eventually and come back. But this time she
seemed to have given up. I got the feeling she didn't believe
that he was ever coming back again. Maybe she didn't
want him to . . .'

But Louie wants his Dad back, and as things get worse
and worse at home, he finally decides he'll have to go and
find him.

Gareth Owen

The Man With Eyes Like Windows

Lions

First published in Great Britain 1987 by
William Collins Sons & Co Ltd
Published in Lions 1988

Lions is an imprint of
the Children's Division, part of
the Collins Publishing Group
8 Grafton Street, London W1X 3LA

Printed in Great Britain by
William Collins Sons & Co. Ltd, Glasgow

For Simon, Ann and Danny

He was standing there beside me
Saw this look come in his eyes
He was looking out the window
But he wasn't seeing skies.

He was in another country
He left me far behind
And though my heart was breaking
I'd pretend I didn't mind.

That's the man with eyes like windows
He just has to wander free
He's looking at a dream he's made
Seeing worlds that you can't see.

Song: The Man with Eyes like Windows
Words and Music by Murray Palermo
From the album 'Murray Palermo The Singer and the Song'
Sunflower Records
Published by Codah Music

He was down there on his own. I couldn't see his face but I knew it was him. There was no doubt about that. I'd know that gangly walk and red lumber jacket anywhere. Why did he walk so slowly? Couldn't he see the danger? He looked so small down there and the concrete face of the dam so enormous. Any second the water was going to burst through. If he could reach the iron ladder he might have a chance. Hurry! Why didn't he hurry? Then the whole dam began to move. It seemed to bell out, then ripple and wave like a gigantic curtain. Tiny cracks appeared and rivulets of water ran down. And still he hadn't seen it. I shouted to him to run but no noise would come out. Huge chunks of masonry, the size of houses, broke free and tumbled slowly down the face of the dam until they broke into a thousand pieces on the concrete floor. And then the water came through. The huge wall ripped open and the water came through in a curving black torrent. At last he's seen it. He turned. His arms went up in horror and he began to run. Why was there no sound? I couldn't understand why there was no sound. All I could hear were his footsteps and the sound of his breathing as he stumbled and ran before that vast wall of water. A first shallow wave knocked him off his feet. Then he was up and running once more. He reached the ladder and began to clamber up desperately. But the water stretched out and plucked him off, and suddenly he was swirling crazily in that black sea amongst the trunks of

7

trees, telegraph poles, the roofs of houses and wildly turning motor cars. For a moment the water twisted him towards me. He was close. I could see the matted hair on the back of his neck. If only he could see me I felt he might be saved. I shouted again but there was still no sound. The branch of a tree caught him and flung him round, his face towards me. But there was nothing. Where his face should have been there was just an emptiness. Why couldn't I see his face? Then it was over. For a moment his head jerked terribly from side to side and suddenly he was gone for ever in all that awful weight of water. I didn't try to scream again. Further off someone else was calling but I couldn't see who it was.

'Dad,' he kept screaming, 'Dad, Dad,' over and over again.

Why did he do that? Why was he calling out for my dad?

There's a light. A bright light shining in my eyes. My mother is in the room beside me. She has her arm around me and Jo is in the doorway, staring. She has her hands over her ears. The screaming is frightening her too. Whoever it is I wish he would stop the screaming. Jo has taken her hands from her ears at last. I've stopped now. I've stopped the screaming. Mum leaves the light on for me. She always does that after a nightmare. I stare at the bedroom ceiling. I think about my dad. I wonder if I saved him. If I managed to save him this time.

Chapter 1

Three months after Dad had run off this last time, I stared at the film on the ceiling but his face wouldn't appear. The more I squinted into the shadows, the less I remembered what he looked like. I don't know when I started. It was just something I'd always done. It was like being in my own private cinema. If I stared long enough and hard enough the shadowy patterns would start to shift and merge and become moving pictures – like the old black and white films Dad used to be in. Before long, Dad's face would appear, winking and smiling, and somehow I'd know that wherever he might be, he would be all right. Once I'd seen his face I'd be able to go to sleep.

I suppose I always imagined him as being in a film because he'd once been an actor in Hollywood. That was before I was born. He wasn't a big star or anything. He was what they call an extra. An extra is somebody they use to fill up the background while the main action is going on somewhere else. He couldn't have made that many films, maybe ten or twelve, but whenever one of them was on we'd all have to go and see it. One of the earliest things I can remember is sitting on Dad's knee in The Majestic and looking up at a huge image of him on the screen. I can only have been about three. He took us to see every film he'd ever been in. We'd go and see the same films over and over again. I was about seven before I realized that Dad wasn't in every picture that had ever been made. The first time I saw a film and he wasn't in it, I thought something must have gone wrong.

Where's Dad? I kept screaming out loud. Where's my dad? I cried so much they had to take me home.

I don't know if you ever saw a film called *Across the San Anton*. He took us to see that ten times. *North West to Wichita* was my favourite. If you ever see that film, watch out for the moment when John Wayne goes into a saloon to shoot this outlaw called Kid Santee. He's been trying to catch him for about ten years because he killed his wife and child and set fire to his ranch, while John Wayne was away winning the Civil War. Kid Santee is leaning on the bar drinking whisky.

John Wayne says to him, 'Kid Santee, I've been looking for you for a long time.'

Kid Santee turns round very slowly and smiles. He's wearing a black eye patch and there's a long scar down his cheek.

He speaks very quietly, 'So now you've found me, what you going to do about it?'

John Wayne walks forward, stepping over a drunk who's lying on the floor. The two men stand still, their hands over their guns. Everybody rushes for cover because they can see there's going to be a fight. Suddenly there's a burst of gun fire and when it clears you see Kid Santee sliding slowly to the ground. John Wayne takes the whisky off the bar and pours it slowly over Santee's face then walks out of the room and rides away. Well, in that scene my Dad was the drunk who's lying on the floor.

Whenever we were in the cinema and one of Dad's scenes was coming up he'd get really excited and start telling us what to look out for in case we missed it.

'It's coming up now,' he'd say. 'Watch out when James

Stewart is buying the cuddly bear for the little blind girl. Keep watching the street outside. Look out for a man wearing a trilby carrying an umbrella and a paper bag.' Well, we'd all lean forward, our eyes glued to the screen on the look out for Dad. When the moment came there'd be about fifty people walking down the street and they all seemed to be wearing hats and carrying umbrellas. It was all over in ten seconds.

'That's me,' Dad would shout so everybody in the cinema could hear. 'Look, that's me.' He'd be really disappointed when we couldn't pick him out. We had to go back and see that film five more times before we could spot him. The manager got to know us quite well.

There was one particular film Dad wanted us to see but it never seemed to come round. Maybe they changed the title. The reason Dad wanted us to see this particular film so badly was because he got to speak a line in it. Extras aren't supposed to speak, otherwise they have to be paid more money. Dad put in this line so that he'd be noticed. If you didn't do something different, he said, you stayed an extra all your life. He knew they wouldn't be able to film the scene again because it was too complicated and expensive. Every day he practised this line he'd made up, trying to say it all kinds of different ways until he'd got it right. Then the big day came. Kirk Douglas has cornered this rustler called Slocum and a few of his men on the top of a cliff. Slocum pretends to be unarmed and shuffles backwards begging for mercy when Kirk Douglas challenges him to a fist fight. 'I guess you got the drop on me this time,' he says, as Kirk walks forward unbuckling his gun belt. One of the outlaws, who's really a goody, sees the gun concealed in Slocum's sleeve and crawls along the cliff behind him so that Slocum stumbles over him and into the ravine. If you ever get to see this film listen really carefully as the men all watch Slocum's body falling. Just before it hits the bottom a voice says, 'Biggest drop I ever saw.' That's the line. That was Dad's line. The trouble was we never found out what the film was called. We had to go and see every Kirk Douglas film hoping we'd hear Dad's line, but we were always disappointed.

Once though, he did get to scream in a film. A scream isn't as good as a line but it's better than walking down a street in the rain carrying an umbrella and a paper bag. In this film there's a big fight in a saloon. After knocking out a few people Burt Lancaster races up some stairs and into a bedroom. On the bed is a greasy cowboy with no trousers firing a gun at the ceiling. Burt picks him up and hurls him through the bedroom window and into a horse trough in the street below. It's as he's falling that Dad gives his scream. He went over the scene again and again with us so as to be sure we didn't miss it. He even gave us a demonstration at home, rolling off the sofa on to the living room carpet to show us what the fall looked like. In the cinema, as the moment for his fall and scream came nearer, I could tell Dad was getting really excited. It was a big moment for him. He leaned forward in his chair rubbing his hands together nervously and drumming his heels on the floor.

'Here it comes,' he whispered, so everyone could hear, 'here comes the scream. Just wait till you hear this scream.' He was chuckling to himself. He even started explaining it to the people in the row behind. 'Watch out for the fall. Watch out for the greasy cowboy with no trousers who falls through the window. That's me.' It was really embarrassing. By the time we got to the fight in the saloon the

12

whole audience was on the look out for the greasy cowboy with no trousers. I was just hoping nobody from my school was there. Well, the fight starts just as Dad told us, but then Burt Lancaster, instead of rushing up the stairs, says, 'Let's get out of here.' The next thing you see he's galloping across the prairie with Maureen O'Hara behind him. For a moment my dad just sat there gazing at the screen with his jaw hanging open. He couldn't believe it. Then he leaped to his feet and started shouting.

'Where's my fall? The bastards cut out my fall.'

Up on the screen Burt Lancaster was kissing Maureen O'Hara in huge close up.

'What do you mean, let's get out of here?' Dad screams at him. 'You're supposed to hit me and I go through the window.'

He turned to the audience, 'They cut my scream. The bastards cut my scream.' The manager had to ask us to leave.

I seemed to spend half my life in the cinema. So perhaps it wasn't surprising that whenever I wanted to remember what my dad looked like, all I'd have to do was stare into the shadows on the bedroom ceiling and there he'd be. Maybe I was dreaming all the time. I don't know. All I can tell is, that these dreams were very real.

Then one night, something terrible happened. The bedroom ceiling turned into a great expanse of snow. Then there was a close-up of a figure lying face down in the snow. I just knew it was my day. I don't know if you ever saw a film called *Snows of Alaska*? Well, it was a bit like that. Two men were looking down at Dad's body. They turned it over. It was awful. Where Dad's face should have been there was just an emptiness. One of the men said, 'Wonder who he was?'

'Just a nobody I guess,' said the other. As the men

walked away I heard one of them say, 'The boy could have saved him; he could have saved him if he'd really wanted.' They walked away into the snow and left the body. I wanted to see Dad's face. I screamed out, 'Dad! Dad,' and woke up covered in sweat. After that, the nightmares happened almost every night. He was always in some kind of danger and I sort of understood that I was being given a chance to save him. All I had to do was remember what his face had been like and then he'd be safe. But I couldn't. I just couldn't make his face come into my mind. I started believing that if he died, somehow it would all be my fault.

I couldn't tell Mum about it because she wouldn't have understood. What made it worse was that the letters stopped coming. Whenever Dad had gone off before there'd always been letters. They weren't like ordinary letters but more like stories. He'd always been a great story teller, my dad. He just made them up as he went along. His letters were just the same. I used to keep them in a box under my bed. Sometimes I'd read them to Jo, my little sister, but then she started getting letters of her own. I loved it when the letter box rattled and those big envelopes with foreign stamps on thumped onto the carpet. We'd tear them open and read bits aloud to one another. It would take you a week to read them properly because he always wrote in tiny handwriting so as to fit as many words as possible on the airmail paper. He'd scribble all down the margins. Half of it would be written upside down and everywhere there were these funny little drawings of this cowboy character Luke Alive that he'd invented.

Sometimes there'd be some money for Mum in the envelope. But that didn't happen very often.

* * *

14

It was frightening not being able to remember Dad's face. The harder I tried the worse it got. I started taking these two photographs to bed to help remind me. The first had been taken about twelve years earlier. It showed Dad standing outside a bar in America wearing a big cowboy hat and carrying a guitar. One afternoon while Mum was at work he'd heard Bob Dylan singing one of his songs on the radio. By the time she got home he'd bought a guitar and had left for America to look for him. That was the kind of thing he was always doing. Of course he never found him. He decided it would be easier to become Bob Dylan. He taught himself to play the guitar and hired himself out singing his own songs in any bar that would let him play. The songs weren't bad but he could hardly play the guitar and his voice wasn't very good, so he was nearly starving when he met Murray P, down in Nashville. Murray could sing but his songs weren't very good. I don't know what Murray P's last name was. That's all Dad ever called him. They got more work together than they did apart. Dad told me a lot of record companies were interested but before they could get anywhere Dad had to come home. I think Murray P. went on to be quite successful. Anyway this photo shows the two of them both wearing big cowboy hats and playing guitars outside a shop. Underneath Dad has written 'Me and Murray P. outside Danby's Store, Nashville, Tenessee'. I liked that photo.

The other photograph was taken on Mum and Dad's wedding day. It always makes me laugh to look at it because everybody on Mum's side of the family looks so miserable. Even the Vicar's looking unhappy and he's paid to look cheerful. There was a reason why Uncle Edgar was looking miserable. He'd wanted to marry Mum himself but Dad heard what he was up to and came rushing back from Hollywood and got in first. Uncle Edgar never forgave Dad for that. In the middle of all these miserable faces stands Dad looking proud and young and sunburnt with a big smile all over his face. So I'd look at these pictures last thing at night but they didn't really help. As soon as I closed my eyes I just couldn't see his face. The feeling started to grow in me that he was dead. Somehow, I just knew that he was dead. I never told anybody about it. Nobody would believe me. I just had to carry this secret around with me all the time. I kept imagining the phone ringing one day and a stranger's voice telling me that my dad was dead. Then they'd know all right; everybody would know.

Then one night it happened. What I had dreaded happened. I was sitting doing my homework. Mum had gone out and Auntie Edith, Uncle Edgar's sister, was baby-sitting Jo. I never liked Auntie Edith much and I don't think she liked me. I don't think she liked anybody. She was using the sewing machine. She always wore this expression as though she'd just swallowed a mouse. Suddenly the phone rang and the noise of it made my skin go cold. Auntie Edith hadn't heard it because of the noise the machine was making, otherwise she'd have picked it up first. She didn't think children should be allowed to anwer phones. As soon as I picked it up she gave me this look. But I didn't care.

A voice said, 'We have a call for you Mrs Langton. Will you pay for the call?' I didn't think, I just said 'Yes'. The line wasn't very clear. The operator must have thought I was Mum. Auntie Edith started hovering round but I wouldn't let her have the phone. It was nothing to do with her.

Then I heard a voice saying, 'Hello Kate.' And it was my dad's voice. At first I couldn't understand how he could be dead and still be able to talk to me. I tried to tell him it wasn't Mum but the words wouldn't come out properly. Then suddenly I started crying. I don't know why, I never usually cry. I could hear Dad asking me what was the matter. I wanted to tell him about the dreams I'd been having and how Mum had let herself get fat since he'd been away; that there was something wrong with her and that when she went into hospital we'd have to go and live with Uncle Edgar until she came out and how Jo had started stealing money and wouldn't talk to anybody. But the words wouldn't come out properly because of the crying. Auntie Edith was trying to get the phone off me but I wouldn't let her. The line was really bad. I asked Dad where he was and what he was doing. He must have understood that because I heard him say that there was money in Palermo. It was very confusing. Auntie Edith was following me round the room saying, 'Is that your father, Louie? Louie, let me speak to him. Give me that phone.' I carried the phone out into the hall and crawled under a big table so she couldn't get at me. And then I realized my dad was crying too. I don't know what the operator must have thought. We were hundreds of miles apart and all she could hear was crying. I asked him where he was. I wanted to know where Palermo was.

Dad said, 'In a phone box.'

I hadn't meant that. I thought of Dad in this phone box in Palermo. I could see it all clearly. It was raining and he was dressed in a trilby and carrying an umbrella like in the James Stewart film. Outside there was a great long queue and they were all shouting and swearing because Dad was taking so long on the phone and all he was doing was crying.

Then Dad said, 'Where are you?'

Without thinking, I said, 'Under the table.' That sounded even funnier than being in a phone box, so we both started laughing at the same time. Then in the middle of all the laughter the line went dead. I didn't even have time to say goodbye.

'Dad, Dad,' I shouted. But he'd gone.

I heard Mum's key in the front door and Jo came down the stairs to meet her in her pyjamas. Auntie Edith said, 'Harold's been on the phone and goodness knows what he said because Louie wouldn't let me speak to him. You really must do something about that boy's behaviour.' It was between me and my dad. It wasn't any of her business. I crawled out from under the table. Auntie Edith was glaring at me. I smiled at her and put the phone back. I didn't care what she thought. I didn't really care what anybody thought.

That was one of the best phone calls I ever had. All we'd done was laugh and cry. But it was one of the best phone calls I'd ever had in my life.

Chapter 2

Why wouldn't anybody tell Jo and me? Everybody else knew. I'd heard Mum and Auntie Edith whispering about it. Even Uncle Edgar knew. Why should he know and not us? He wasn't family. One afternoon after school I asked Auntie Edith straight out, 'Why is Mum going into hospital?' All she did was purse up her lips as though another mouse had just disappeared and say, 'Little pigs have big ears.' She was full of little sayings like that, was Auntie Edith. Whenever she thought you'd done something wrong, out would pop another one. 'Go to the ant, thou sluggard.' That was another one of hers. I didn't know what a sluggard was but it didn't sound much better than a pig to me. She wouldn't like it if I called her a pig. I was dreading living at her house while Mum was in hospital.

I couldn't help thinking that if Dad had been around Mum wouldn't even have been taken ill. In a way, I suppose she'd got used to Dad running off. She knew he'd get fed up eventually and come back. But this time she seemed to have given up. I got the feeling she didn't believe that he was ever coming home again. Maybe she didn't want him to. She'd started to get really fat. As if she didn't care any more. And sometimes I'd get home from school and she'd still be wandering round in her housecoat and the breakfast plates would still be on the table. She'd never have done that if Dad had been around. The feeling started to grow inside me that if only I could find out where he was I'd tell him all about it and that would make him want to come back home.

Mum was really miserable when the time came for us to leave the hospital. She just sat on the bed holding on to this big suitcase. It had Dad's initials painted on it in big white letters. I could see she wanted to hang on to it when the nurse came to take it away. Mum tried to smile as she gave us both a hug but I could tell she was really unhappy. She whispered to me, 'Try to be good for Uncle Edgar and Auntie Edith.' I think she was crying a bit. But she pretended she wasn't. Jo didn't want to go at all. She started screaming, 'Mummy, Daddy!' so that all the ward could hear. She hung on to the bars at the bottom of Mum's bed and wouldn't let go. Uncle Edgar started going pink and looking round as if he was really embarrassed. 'Dear me, what a display,' he kept muttering. Jo wasn't embarrassed. She screamed the place down. In the end they had to fetch two nurses to prise her fingers off the bed rails. Then she went completely quiet and wouldn't talk to anybody. As we walked through the car park towards Uncle Edgar's car I looked up and saw Mum watching us from a third storey window. She waved. I felt stupid somehow, waving in front of a load of people. Before waving back, I looked round to see if anybody was watching. Then I felt rotten. Mum wouldn't have worried what anybody else thought. So then I gave this great big wave. I didn't care who saw. Uncle Edgar said, 'For goodness sake!'

As we drove into the street I closed my eyes. I looked out of the window so nobody would see. I didn't want Uncle Edgar to think I was crying or anything. I tried to make a picture in my head of Mum waving. I thought if I could see her she'd be all right. Then it started changing into one of my films. Mum was standing by the window just like I'd seen her. She was crying now because she knew we weren't there to see her. There was a huge crashing sound. It was Jo playing with the action man Dad had bought her the Christmas before. She kept making bazooka and machine gun noises with her mouth. Jo was really good at noises. I felt it was important that Jo should be able to see Mum too.

I said to her, 'You have to close your eyes and see Mum waving. Like the last time you saw her.' Jo stuck out her bottom lip and shook her head.

Uncle Edgar half looked round. 'What's all the whispering?'

'Nothing,' I said. I said to Jo, 'You have to do it. It's important.'

Jo screwed her eyes up really hard.

'Can you still see her?' I asked.

'No,' she said and flung her action man so hard that it landed on the front seat next to Uncle Edgar.

'Kerblaam,' she shouted. I could tell Uncle Edgar didn't like the way Jo was behaving but he was trying to be friendly. Somehow though, it didn't work. Uncle Edgar is one of these people who can't help being frightening. It's something to do with his face. He has this very soft skin that looks as if he doesn't have to shave and he wears these gold rim spectacles. The worst thing is the way his face used to shake. Every time he spoke or even looked at you, his face would shiver slightly as though he was really angry inside and it was all ready to burst out. Not angry like Dad, who swore and threw things all over the place. Uncle Edgar just spoke very quietly and coldly, and all the time his head would be going shake, shake, shake. Maybe he has bad nerves. I don't know. I don't mind telling you I was a bit frightened of Uncle Edgar. Anyway, he was trying his best to be friendly. He could understand that we were both upset about leaving Mum in hospital. He handed the action man back to Jo.

'Here's your doll,' he said. Jo snatched it and flung it into the back of the car making a mortar bomb sound. The spit came out of her mouth. Uncle Edgar flinched. He looked at us in the mirror. I could see his gold specs going shake, shake, shake. He smiled at Jo.

'And what do you want to be when you grow up?' he asked.

'A commando,' said Jo, without looking up.

Uncle Edgar coughed into his fist and drove on.

I stared out of the car window. I wondered what Dad would be doing at that exact moment. I read in a book once how two people could be locked in a room miles apart and could still think of the same thing if they concentrated hard enough. I liked the idea of doing that. I concentrated hard and tried to imagine what Dad might be doing in Palermo. Nothing would come into my head. Then one of my films started. Mum was sitting on the hospital bed with a suitcase beside her. Suddenly the lid opened and Dad came out wearing a cowboy hat and carrying a guitar. He held out his arms and bowed, smiling, as if there was an audience. Mum laughed too and went to put her arms round him but he suddenly went flat and slid under the door.

'You don't have to worry.'

I woke up with a start. Uncle Edgar was speaking to me.

'I said you mustn't worry too much. Your mother will be out in a week,' he said. 'It's nothing serious.'

'What's wrong with her?' I asked. They still hadn't told me.

22

Uncle Edgar waved his hand. 'You wouldn't understand. One of these things women have.'

I didn't know what women have. Why didn't he try and tell me. She was my mum. There was a silence. I wondered where Palermo was. Uncle Edgar cleared his throat.

'Penny for them,' he said. What business was it of his what I was thinking about?

'Nothing,' I said. Uncle Edgar pressed a button and the front window slid down. He threw a cigarette out into the street. It was raining.

'Oh I'd forgotten,' he said, 'there's a surprise visitor waiting for you at home.'

Jo stopped playing with her action man. 'Daddy,' she said. 'Is Daddy coming home?'

Uncle Edgar shook his head and smiled. 'No, no it's not your Daddy. Your Daddy's gone on holiday'. That was another lie. We both knew Dad had run off. Why didn't anybody ever tell the truth. 'It's Billy. Billy's home from school. I expect you'll have lots to talk about.'

Billy was Uncle Edgar's son. I used to go round with him when we were in the Junior School but we hadn't really got on since I knocked one of his front teeth out. It hadn't been a real fight. Dad had taken us to see a midweek international and left us with enough money to go into the boys' enclosure. We'd only been about nine at the time. When we went to go through the turnstile we found out we had to pay full price because it was a midweek game. Billy went mad and started shouting at me, saying that if his Dad had been there he would have made sure we'd got in first. He went on and on about it. In the end I lost my temper. All I could see was Billy's mouth open and closing and all these words coming out. So I hit him as hard as I could. The words stopped suddenly and his tooth was on

23

the floor instead of being in his mouth. I was sorry straight away because he was my best pal at the time. In the ground there was a big roar, I suppose England must have scored. Billy was on his hands and knees looking for his tooth. His face was red and there was blood on his lips.

Suddenly he got up and started circling round me with his fists up saying, 'Come on, now you're for it,' over and over again. Every time I went to hit him he just whirled away out of range. I said he could have the money and go in on his own. But he wouldn't. In the end I went in. It seemed daft for neither of us to see the match. After about ten minutes I looked round and I could see him in the crowd behind me. He must have had enough money all the time. I waved for him to come down but he just held up his fist and screwed up his face. I could read his lips. He was saying, 'You wait. I'll get you.' He never did though. After that we never spoke to each other much. We'd sometimes pass in the corridor at school but he would never speak. I'd been mates with him for about five years but I didn't really like him. Because he was my cousin we'd sometimes have to talk when we all went to his house for tea. He'd always find a chance to say, 'Where's that money your dad owes me for the football match?' That was typical of Billy. He never forgot anything. Anyway, when he was ten his Dad made him leave Mary Street and he went to a private school, so I didn't see him so much after that. We didn't seem to have much to say to one another. Not like when he was eight and had to go to a psychiatrist.

He wasn't mad. It was just after his Mum, my Auntie Joyce, died and he developed this stutter because he wasn't getting on with his Dad. I couldn't understand how his dad could make him stutter but that's what the psychiatrist said. To tell you the truth, I liked him better when he was mad. Every Wednesday morning he used to sit at the back of Miss Mellor's class and tell me all these mad questions this doctor had asked him the night before. I really looked forward to Wednesdays. That's how he got the name Billy Fa Fa, because of his stutter. Mr Loveridge, our Headmaster, was asking everybody in our class what they wanted to be when they grew up. Billy put his hand up. He was one of these kids who always has his hand up. He was trying to say that he wanted to work in this Mother and Baby store that his dad owned. But when he tried to say 'father' all that came out was 'fa fa fa fa'. After that, everybody called him Billy Fa Fa. It stuck. Even after the psychiatrist cured his stutter he was still known as Billy Fa Fa. He hated it. If I ever wanted to annoy him all I had to do was call him Fa Fa.

We climbed out of the car and walked up the drive. Auntie Edith was standing in the doorway wiping her hands on a pinafore. I couldn't see Billy Fa Fa. I was relieved he wasn't there, although I knew we'd have to meet sooner or later. As their front door slammed shut I felt like a prisoner who was starting a long sentence. I remembered my promise to Mum. I whispered to Jo, 'Be as good as you can.' She just looked at me. You could never tell with Jo.

It wasn't easy keeping out of trouble at Uncle Edgar's. They seemed to have so many rules. Even if you were standing about doing nothing you got the feeling you were doing something wrong. Everything was so clean you didn't like to touch anything. Jo sat down on a funny little chair by the window and straight away Auntie Edith was there with a tight little smile. 'Oh Josephine darling, we don't sit on that chair.' That was something I noticed

25

about Auntie Edith, she always said 'we'. 'We're going to make our beds before breakfast, aren't we?' Or, 'We'd like to go to Sunday School this afternoon.' Or 'We should have washed our hands before coming to table.' All the time 'we'. No wonder Billy Fa Fa had to see a psychiatrist. Just as I was thinking about him he wandered in through the french windows. He was wearing shorts. I couldn't stop looking at his long thin legs. Since I'd seen him the last time he'd grown brown hair all over them. I'd never seen legs like them. He just walked past me and took out this book on astronomy and started reading it as though it was dead interesting. But I could tell he wasn't really reading. I thought I'd try to be polite since we were in his house.

'Good book?' I asked. He didn't even look up. Just carried on reading. That was typical of him.

'Be like that,' I said. It suited me fine if he didn't want to talk. Jo was staring at Fa Fa's legs.

'Funny legs,' she said.

Billy gave her a look but he didn't say anything.

I got my own back at the tea table though. I couldn't help it. Having tea with Uncle Edgar and Auntie Edith was like going to the dentist. You all had to be sitting quiet before the meal came in and then they had grace. They had grace before every meal even though it wasn't Sunday. You had to say 'please' and 'thank you' all the time. And you couldn't leave the table until you'd eaten a plain piece of bread. I was determined to make Billy talk. So I kept asking him to pass me things. I was really polite. He couldn't do anything about it because his dad was there. All through the meal I kept saying: 'Could I have the butter please, Billy?' and 'Would you kindly pass the lettuce please, Billy?' I could see he was getting mad passing these things up and down the table. After a bit Jo realized what I was up to and she started. 'Could I have some more lemonade, Billy please?' Billy's arms must have been getting tired. Auntie Edith was beaming. 'Our manners are improving,' she said. Jo couldn't help giggling. She nearly got me started. Uncle Edgar gave her a look and said, 'Quiet Times.' This meant no one was allowed to speak for five minutes. That's when the trouble started. The longer it went on the more I wanted to laugh. I daren't catch Jo's eye. That would have been the end. All you could hear was munching sounds and the clink of knives and forks. Sometimes Uncle Edgar would ask for milk or sugar and that was the most exciting thing that happened. I couldn't help watching Auntie Edith's lips going in circles as she chewed. I thought, there goes another mouse. I wondered if Jo was thinking the same thing. This laugh started rumbling at the bottom of my stomach. To put it off, I started to think of executions and people having their legs chopped off but the laughter wouldn't go away. I stared into my plate. It was like when you start giggling in church or when one of the teachers is telling you off. Or like that time at Auntie Joyce's funeral when I couldn't stop laughing. Just then Jo gave a really loud belch. I couldn't help looking at her. She was looking surprised as if she was wondering where this loud noise had come from. The laugh wouldn't stay down. I tried to change it into a cough and started choking. I could feel Uncle Edgar looking at me over his rimless specs.

'Manners,' Auntie Edith said.

I was shaking with laughter but no sound was coming out. What finished me though was when Auntie Edith said, 'Very nice leg on this chicken.' I couldn't help it. I started thinking of Billy Fa Fa. I got a sudden picture of him running around a farmyard with chicken legs. Jo caught my eye and I knew she was thinking the same. A great coughing roar came out and I just couldn't stop. Then Jo started. They made us finish our tea in the kitchen on our own. I kept trying to be serious and telling Jo how she'd promised to behave but then I'd start laughing again. I don't think Auntie Edith and Uncle Edgar liked laughing. Jo couldn't eat her salad. She slipped it into the rubbish bin but Auntie Edith found it and gave us a long lecture on how wrong it was to waste food and that if Jo didn't eat up her lettuce they'd send it to Africa where there were lots of children who'd be grateful for it. Jo started arguing back saying lettuce made her sick and that it wouldn't do any good sending it to Africa anyway because by the time it got there the lettuce would have gone limp. I tried to stop her but Jo is very determined once she gets going. Auntie Edith started going pink around her neck. She wasn't used to being argued with. She called Jo 'a defiant little madam.' Jo started to cry and then was sick all over the kitchen floor. She was sent to bed early.

I had to sleep in the same room as Billy Fa Fa. For about an hour I stared at the ceiling pretending to be asleep. I hated sleeping in the same room as him. Suddenly out of the blue he says, 'If you think I've forgotten about that three quid your dad owes me you've got another think coming.' I couldn't believe it.

'That was years ago, Fa Fa,' I said.

'Don't call me Fa Fa,' he said. There was a silence. I could hear him breathing. I had five pounds in my pocket that Mum had given me and Jo. Even though I didn't feel I owed him anything, I thought I'd give him the three pounds out of that five just to keep him quiet.

28

'I'll give it to you now and then maybe you'll shut up about it,' I said.

'I don't want it off you. It's your dad owes it me.' He turned over. 'Not much chance of getting it off him, is there? Gone off again, hasn't he? How many times is that? Four?'

'Who says he's run off?'

'Good riddance. He's not coming back this time.'

'Who says he's not coming back?'

'Me Dad says so.' This was one of Fa Fa's favourite phrases. If you ever had an argument with him he always ended it by saying, 'Me Dad says so.'

'Well that's where you're wrong, Fa Fa.' He knew he'd got me mad. He was enjoying all this.

'All right then, where is he?' He sneered.

I looked up into the darkness. 'Palermo', I said. 'He's in Palermo if you really want to know.'

'Palermo. What's he doing in Palermo?'

I didn't know what he was doing. I didn't even know where Palermo was. 'Why should I tell you. Anyway you don't know where Palermo is.'

'Who says?'

'I say.' I knew he wouldn't be able to resist telling me.

'Everybody knows. It's in Italy. If you went to a decent school you'd learn something.'

So that's where Dad was. What was he doing in Italy?

It was as if Billy had heard my thoughts.

'What's he doing in Italy? I suppose he's going to be the next Pope. It'll be the first time they've had a liar for Pope.'

I could hear the sound of the television coming up through the floor.

'He's making a film, Fa Fa.'

'Oh yeah,' said Billy scornfully. 'Like those crappy films

29

he made years ago. One blink and you missed him. You're a bleeding liar, Langton. You're a liar, just like your Dad.'

I'd had enough. I got up. It was pitch black. I could hear Fa Fa's bed clothes rustling. He was trying to see where I was.

'Don't you touch me, Langton, I'll tell my dad.' I stood dead quiet for about ten seconds. 'What are you doing?' He was getting really nervous.

'I'm going to kill you, Fa Fa,' I said in a whisper. I crept out of the bedroom taking the blankets with me. Out on the landing I could hear him saying, 'Langton? Langton where are you?'

I opened the door of Jo's bedroom. The moon was flooding through the room. Jo was lying curled up in a ball with her thumb in her mouth and her eyes wide open.

'Are you asleep?' I asked.

'Yes,' she said.

There was a couch against the window. I lay down and wrapped the blankets round me. I wondered if Billy was still waiting to be killed. I could hear Uncle Edgar's voice through the floorboards. Now and then Auntie Edith's higher voice came in. You couldn't make out any words though, just the sounds of their voices.

'Hear that?' I said. 'I bet they're talking about us.'

Jo still had her thumb in her mouth. She was resting her forefinger along her nose. Her big eyes were staring at me without blinking.

'I hate her,' she said, without taking her thumb out. 'I hate him too.' She paused. 'I was naughty, wasn't I?'

'Yes, you were.'

'I know,' she said, and smiled.

I remembered my promise to Mum.

'They're doing their best,' I said.

'Why did you come in here?' she asked.

'I couldn't stand being with Billy.'

'Why?'

'He kept saying things about Dad.'

'Why?'

'I don't know why.' I turned over and looked out of the window. There was a big round moon shining over the trees. It reminded me of being high up somewhere. High up and safe. There was a banging noise from Jo's bed.

'What you doing?' I asked.

'Hitting the pillow,' she said. 'I'm imagining it's Auntie Edith.' There were more bangs. 'That was Uncle Edgar.' The banging stopped. 'They're both dead now. Shall I kill Billy as well?'

'Go to sleep,' I said. I heard her bed creaking. The next second her face was right over mine.

'I want a drink of water.'

'Don't tell me. Go and get one.'

I heard her going down the stairs and the sound of water running. Then she was back. I heard her gulping the water. She gasped.

'I did a wee at the same time.'

'Good.'

'I heard them talking,' she said.

'Who?'

'You know. Uncle and Auntie of course. I heard what they were saying.'

'How?'

'Put my ear to the door.'

'You shouldn't have done that. You shouldn't listen to other people's conversations. What did they say?'

'She was talking about Mum.'

'What was she saying about Mum?'

31

'Auntie Edith said she ought to get divorced.'

'Divorced?'

Jo gulped some more water down. 'What did she mean?'

'Nothing. Go to sleep.'

'Does it mean Dad's not coming back?'

'Of course he's coming back. Do you miss Dad?'

'I don't think he's coming back.'

I could almost feel her thinking. After a pause she said, 'You know what I miss? I miss my climbing frame. Can't we go home tomorrow and do gymnastics?'

'Go to sleep,' I said.

'What do you miss? Louie, what do you miss most of all in the world?'

'I don't know,' I said.

I was thinking about the time we'd all gone to that Country and Western Club in town and Dad had been given a box of glasses for winning the fast draw competition. He'd worn a stetson and a green and black shirt. He'd sung one of his songs. He didn't sing very well but they all clapped and cheered. Mum had worn a long dress with frills and a straw hat that hung round her neck by a string. Afterwards they'd danced round together to one of those old fashioned waltzes. It seemed like a long time ago.

'You know what I miss?' I said softly to Jo.

There was no answer. She was fast asleep.

Chapter 3

I knew something was wrong the minute we arrived back from visiting Mum. Auntie Edith was waiting for us by the front gate. She ran over to the car and shouted through the window.

'It's Jo,' she said. 'What shall we do?' She began to cry. Uncle Edgar got out of the car.

'What's happened?' he asked sternly.

'It's Jo,' said Auntie Edith.

'Where is she?'

'That's just it. I don't know. I only left here for five minutes. We had a little row. She's not an easy child. She'd been watching some television programme. I don't know. I didn't think it was suitable so I turned it off. She started to sulk. Then she seemed to get over it. I went into the garden to bring the clothes in. When I came back she was gone.'

'Have you looked round the house?'

'Yes, of course.'

Uncle Edgar strode down the garden. 'Have you looked in the garden?'

'Yes. Yes. Everywhere.'

Uncle Edgar was walking round the garden shouting out for Jo.

'Next door? Have you asked next door?' he said to Auntie Edith.

'Yes, and opposite. Oh Edgar, it's all my fault I . . .' Auntie Edith started sniffling again.

33

'Of course it's not your fault, Edith. The child's just out of hand. It doesn't help to cry, Edith.'

Auntie Edith dabbed at her eyes.

'I'm sorry. But what if something's happened to her. You hear such dreadful things.'

'Let's take a look in the house. She could be hiding somewhere, just to frighten you. She's that sort of a child. How long has she been gone?'

'About fifty minutes. I tried to ring you at the hospital. Do you think we ought to tell the police?'

Uncle Edgar ran his fingers through his hair and wrinkled his brow.

'I think we'd better. Where can she have got to?'

I suddenly remembered what Jo had said four nights ago. About missing her gymnastic frame. I knew where she'd be. I brushed past Uncle Edgar and ran towards the gate.

'Eh, where are you off to?' he shouted.

'I know where she's gone,' I shouted. I was down the road running. I looked back and saw the two of them standing by the front gate and then I was round the corner and into Adison Road. There was no one at the bus stop. How often did the buses run? I didn't know. I looked back up the road. It was empty. I didn't want Uncle Edgar catching up with me in his car. I thought, everybody was leaving me. Dad then Mum and now Jo. It was starting to rain. A car approached. I stuck my thumb out but it rushed past, the tyres making a sizzling noise in the rain. I decided to run for it. It was nearly half a mile to our house. She might have got tired and stopped on the way. I turned up my collar against the rain and jogged towards Station Road. Half way between the two stops a bus trundled by. I waved to the driver to stop but he took no notice. I took

34

a short cut through the back of Livsey's, the coal merchant, and out on to the main road. I felt the coldness of the front door key in my trouser pocket. Mum had wanted me to fetch something from the house for her. It was a fabric picture she'd been doing. She'd wanted to finish it while she was in hospital. It would help to pass the time. That showed she must be feeling better. The station gates were closed. I ran over the bridge. The train rattled past underneath me. I thought, What if I'm wrong? What if Jo's not there? She must have had a terrible row with Auntie Edith. She'd never run off before. Dad was the only one in our family who was always running away. I wondered if she might have gone to the hospital. But that was four miles away. Jo wouldn't know that though.

I was in our street. It was funny seeing it after not being there for a few days. Mrs Delaney was putting some milk bottles out.

'Hello Louie, how's your mum?' she called out.

'Better thanks, Mrs Delaney.'

'That's right. When's she coming home?'

'Sunday, I think.'

'It's very quiet without you all. Brought the good weather with you I see.' She went inside.

I ran to our side gate but it was locked. I shouted through the gate.

'Jo, Jo,' I shouted as soon as I was inside. I heard a radio playing somewhere. I went to the front door; turned the key in the lock. I'd have to phone Uncle Edgar so he could get the police. If she wasn't at home where could she be? I couldn't help wondering if something had happened to her. The film in my head started. I could see her lying face down in a pool of water with her arms stretched out. I started to shiver.

'Jo, Jo,' I shouted as soon as I was inside. I heard my own voice coming back at me. It felt strange being in the house with nobody there. The curtains were drawn but Mum had left a light on in the living room and the hallway. I went upstairs and into Mum and Dad's bedroom. I put on the light. Some of Mum's clothes were laid out neatly on the bed. The fabric picture was exactly where she'd said it would be; against the window. It was based on a photograph taken at the old house. We were all walking down a hillside through a cornfield towards the house under a full moon. Mum had been working on it for a long time. But something was different about it. Where Dad had been, there was just a space. His picture had been unpicked. It reminded me of my dream. I hoped Mum was going to put Dad back into it.

I walked towards the bedroom door with the picture rolled up under my arm. On the dressing table was a strip of photos. The kind you get done in a booth. It showed four shots of Mum and Dad. They must have been taken a few days before he left this last time. Mum looked the same in every photo. She was looking straight at the camera with this calm, half smile on her face. Dad was fooling about like he always did. In the first one he seemed to be looking past the camera. As if there was something out there that only he could see. Then he was smiling. Then pulling a really sad face. In the last one he had one hand up over his face as though he was waving goodbye. I felt there was something strange about that last picture but I couldn't make out what it was. Then I realized. It was the index finger on Dad's right hand. The nail was grown really long.

Leaning against the wardrobe was his guitar case. It was all cracked and stained and had lots of labels stuck all over it. I opened it up but there was no guitar inside. Then I heard something. At first I thought I was dreaming. That radio I thought I'd heard. It was playing one of Dad's songs. He'd sung it to us hundreds of times. I could even make out the words. I knew it by heart.

> I've travelled in so many places
> I've wandered far and wide
> Promised you I'd come back some day
> You weren't to know that I had lied.

I couldn't work it out. Nobody else knew about that song except Dad. How could anybody be singing it on the radio? I yanked open the curtains and peered out. The garden looked to be empty. But you couldn't see clearly because of the trees. I could still hear the song though. It seemed to be coming from the garden shed. The door was ajar. And yet I was certain I'd closed it tight before we left. Then something else caught my eye. Behind the crab apple tree. Something was swinging slowly backwards and forwards. There was a piece of material. I couldn't quite make it out. Like a piece of rag. Or a frock . . .

'Jo!' I screamed. I jumped down the stairs three at a time and through the front door. The side gate was locked. I scrambled up and flung myself over, scratching my hands and knees. Please don't let her have done anything, I was saying to myself. Please God let her be alive. Jo's face was upside down. Her hair was brushing the ground as she swung backwards and forwards. Her eyes were closed.

'Jo,' I said.

'I can swing like this upside down for five minutes,' she said. She was hanging by her knees from the gymnastic frame that was bolted on to the crab apple tree. She opened her eyes. Her face was pink.

'You look ever so funny upside down,' she said.

'Jo,' I said, 'I thought you'd . . .' I was so relieved I got angry.

'What you mean by going off like that? Auntie Edith'll kill you.'

'I don't care,' said Jo. 'I don't like her.'

'That doesn't matter. How did you get here?'

'I walked.'

'It's over half a mile. Don't you ever do that again.' I was beginning to sound like Auntie Edith.

'I walked in the rain. It was jolly nice. I liked it.' She swung herself up on to her feet. 'I'm going to do it again tomorrow.'

'You must promise never to run away again.'

'Do we have to go back? I want to stay here.'

'Of course we have to go back? Uncle Edgar's worried sick. The police may be looking for you. Didn't you hear me calling?'

'I couldn't because of the music. Anyway you don't hear as well upside down.'

The music. I'd forgotten about that. It had stopped now. I'd been so worried about Jo I'd forgotten.

'I heard singing,' I said. 'Did you hear it?'

'Yes of course, silly.'

'It was one of Dad's songs. They're silly songs.'

'Who was it, Jo?'

She had run off after Mrs Delaney's cat that had crept through the hedge. She crouched low and began to stroke it.

It was getting dark. I could hear Jo talking to the cat.

38

She chased it down the garden squealing softly. I pushed open the door of the shed. Inside it was murky and smelled of peat, turpentine, paint and old sacks. It was empty. On the workbench a tiny green light gleamed. It was Dad's cassette player. Jo must have put the tape on. I pressed 'rewind' and then 'play'. It started in the middle of the song. It was Dad's song all right but it wasn't Dad singing. The cassette cover was lying on the bench. I couldn't see it clearly in the gloom. I picked up a torch and switched it on. On the cover was a photograph of a fat man wearing a cowboy hat and singing into a microphone. Jo ran up and stood panting in the doorway.

'It's not Dad,' I said.

'I know that,' she said.

'Why is somebody else singing Dad's song?'

I looked at the cover again. Above the picture was written *Country Songs* and underneath *The Best of Murray Palermo*.

I read it twice. That's who Murray P. was.

'It wasn't a place, after all.'

'What place?' asked Jo.

'You remember, I had that phone call from Dad. I thought he said he was in Palermo. But he wasn't. He was talking about this man.'

I turned over the cassette. On the back was a list of songs. I ran my finger down. *Crazy. But I love You* was the third one down. It didn't mention Dad's name. Underneath was written *All Songs written by Murray Palermo*.

'But Dad wrote that.'

'Wrote what?' asked Jo.

'That song. Dad wrote it. Why hasn't he got his name after it? If Dad wrote the song it should have his name after it.'

I switched off the machine and slipped the cassette into my pocket. I don't suppose it mattered that Murray Palermo was singing Dad's song. Maybe Dad hadn't written it in the first place. I was beginning to wonder if Dad had lied about a lot of things.

Jo shivered. 'I'm cold,' she said.

I took her small hand in mine.

'Come on,' I said. 'Let's go and phone Uncle Edgar.'

I walked her across the lawn. The rain had stopped and the dark sky was clear. Jo stopped and pointed upwards. 'Look at the moon,' she said.

'Some people go mad when the moon's full,' I said.

'Is that why I ran away?' I squeezed her hand.

I thought of Mum's fabric picture, the strip of photographs and the empty guitar case. It was like being a detective. I had all the clues but I couldn't put them all together. Then it came to me. That's why his fingernail had been long. It had been long like that when he'd come home from America. I remembered him telling me that guitar players often grew that fingernail long so they could play the guitar better. When that photo had been taken he must have been planning to go away. You couldn't grow your nail like that in a couple of weeks. He must have known about it for months. He must have known all that time and he hadn't told Mum or Jo or me. How could he have done that to us? Dad was out there somewhere playing his guitar with Murray Palermo while Mum was ill in hospital. Jo was running away and I was having to put up with Uncle Edgar, Auntie Edith and Billy. It wasn't fair. That was the first time I'd thought anything like that about Dad. I picked up the phone and dialled Uncle Edgar's number.

40

'Maybe he'll feel sorry for us and come and fetch us in his car,' I said.

'I'll cry if you like,' said Jo. 'I can cry any time I want to.' Her face began to crumple and her lower lip shivered.

'I know,' I said.

Jo took the phone from me.

'It's me,' she shouted. 'It's Jo.'

I heard Uncle Edgar's voice asking where she was.

'I'm here,' she shouted.

I took the phone from her.

I said, 'It's me, Louie. I've got Jo. We're at home.'

Chapter 4

Ten days later Mum came out of hospital. It was a relief to be out of Uncle Edgar's and back in our own home again. Mum was paler and thinner than she'd been before but she seemed to have more energy. Uncle Edgar came round quite often to see that she was all right. Sometimes he came with Auntie Edith but a lot of the time he came on his own. It seemed to cheer Mum up. Jo hated him coming round. She did everything she could to annoy him. One night on Mum's birthday Uncle Edgar arranged to take her out to dinner in a big restaurant. Mum was really looking forward to it. It was years since she'd been taken out for a meal. Dad could never afford it. She bought a new dress and had her hair done. She looked really nice. Jo hated her going out. All afternoon she stayed in her room sulking. She even pretended to be ill so that Mum wouldn't be able to go out. I didn't know what was the matter with her. Then, when the time came for them to leave, they couldn't get into the car. Jo had hidden Uncle Edgar's keys. He tried everything to get her to tell him where she'd put them. But she wouldn't. At first he pretended to make a joke of it. Then he tried being serious and reasonable. But that didn't do any good either. In the end he really lost his temper and started shouting. That frightened Jo. She ran upstairs and hid in Mum's wardrobe. When I opened the door all I could see were these two big eyes staring out at me from amongst the coats and dresses. She reminded me of a hunted animal.

By the time Uncle Edgar found the keys it was too late to go and eat. He was really furious. After that whenever Jo heard Uncle Edgar's car pulling into the drive she'd run straight upstairs and hide in the wardrobe. In the end she was practically living in there. Uncle Edgar realized he'd upset Mum by shouting at Jo. So he tried to make it up to us by being extra nice. Every now and then he'd take us out on a special treat. They can't have been much fun for him. Jo wouldn't speak and I was spending more and more of my time day dreaming. I just couldn't help it.

One day Uncle Edgar took us all out for a picnic at Hemsley Woods. Jo wasn't speaking to anybody, not even me. She wouldn't even look out of the car window. Uncle Edgar was trying like mad to be friendly. He'd point at interesting places on the way but Jo just stared straight ahead, her lower lip stuck straight out. We drove along in silence for a while then Mum and Uncle Edgar started whispering, thinking we couldn't hear, the way that adults do sometimes. Mum was apologizing for Jo's behaviour.

Uncle Edgar said, 'What she needs is a stable background.'

'I suppose so,' said Mum.

'It's just a stage she's going through,' said Uncle Edgar. 'She'll grow out of it once she's got used to the idea.'

I wondered what it was that Jo and I were supposed to get used to. Jo had heard everything too.

'I'm not going through a stage,' she said. 'I'm going to be like this always.'

When we arrived at the picnic place, it started raining. We sat in the car in silence, eating our sandwiches and watching the water trickle down the windows. It wasn't a very cheerful day out.

On the way home I closed my eyes and pretended I was

asleep. The film started in my head. For some reason I started thinking about the time when I was five years old and Dad had a job with a tour company, driving coaches. He used to drive all over the country and sometimes he'd take me with him. The part I liked best was when we drove home empty, after dropping off all the passengers. Dad would start doing mad commentaries through this microphone he had or singing some of his songs. This one night it was pelting it down with rain as we drove home, empty. We turned down Monument Street where the bus terminus was. There was a great long queue of people waiting in the rain for a bus. They were soaked. Dad couldn't stand to see all these people queuing up in the rain so he stopped and picked them all up. He wasn't supposed to. Only council buses were supposed to do that. The bus was packed. Everybody was steaming and there was a smell of wet raincoats. We'd never had the bus so crowded. All the way home he was singing his songs and soon everybody was joining in. The whole bus was singing. He dropped everybody off near their front gates. That was the best bus trip I'd ever been on. Of course Dad got the sack. Somebody must have told the bus company what he'd been up to. It was all in the papers. Dad even had his picture on the front page of *The Argus*.

He was leaning out of his cabin window giving the thumbs up sign and smiling. Underneath was written in big letters *The Singing Bus Driver*. It wasn't long after that that he ran away to America to look for Bob Dylan. It was while he was away that time that Jo had been born. Mum wasn't able to work. She had to sell our old house and borrow money off Uncle Edgar to buy another one. By the time Dad had heard about the baby and the house it was all too late. I don't think Mum ever forgave him for that.

44

It was difficult though to stay angry with Dad for long. Mum used to say about him, 'One thing about your Dad, he's crazy but I love him.' It became a catch phrase in our house. Later on Dad used it in a song.

I opened my eyes and looked out of the window. We were driving past the old house. I could see the hole in the hedge where the bus had gone through that time I'd been playing in the cabin while Dad was having his tea. I must have let the brake off because the bus started rolling backwards down the hill. I was only five. I was so scared that I ran into this field behind the house. The corn came over my head. It was like being in a yellow forest. I was too frightened to go home. I began to cry, then I lay down in the middle of the corn and fell asleep. When I woke up I didn't know where I was. There was a big round white thing in the sky. I reached out to touch it but I couldn't reach. It was the moon. Then Dad's face was there. He reached down and pulled me up, high up on to his shoulders. We went back home with me up there, high up and safe . . . The moon was over our shoulders. We seemed to be towing it behind us like a white balloon.

I said to Mum, 'Look, there's the hole in the hedge where I drove the bus through that time.' But she wouldn't look. She hated going past that house and seeing somebody else living there. She'd loved that house. She pulled Jo up on her knee and looked out of the window on the other side.

Uncle Edgar turned round towards Mum. 'Eight o'clock all right for dinner tonight?'

Mum kept looking out of the window but she was smiling when she said, 'That sounds very nice.'

I had this feeling that even if Dad did come back she

wouldn't want to see him again. That he'd let her down too many times.

A week later came the fire and I knew that something had to be done.

I couldn't believe that Sheila Whiteley was cycling down our street. I'd been in love with her ever since I'd seen her on the train that day coming home from school. She'd been with two of her pals. I hadn't been able to stop looking at her. She didn't know though, because I was pretending to gaze out of the window, but all the time I was looking at her reflection in the glass. She had this skin that looked as if it was blushing all the time and she always seemed to be smiling, even when she wasn't. Her reflection was all mixed up with the trees and buildings that were flashing past. It made me feel funny; like ill and nervous and excited all at the same time. I decided to give her this look I'd been practising. It was a look I'd seen Robert Mitchum giving in *The Devil to Pay*. There had been a great back view of Dad in that picture, walking away after delivering a letter to Robert Mitchum's mum.

It took a lot of concentration to get his look just right. You had to use your eyebrows a lot as if you were frowning but keep half smiling with your mouth. You couldn't keep it going for too long otherwise it made your face ache. One of Sheila Whiteley's friends was messing around with a tennis racket, pretending it was a frying pan. They were all laughing. Just as Sheila Whiteley's head came round I gave her the look full blast, but she didn't see because she was looking down the corridor. I started moving my head around to attract her attention. The look was beginning to give me a headache. At Fairfield station they all stood up to get off. As the three of them went past my window I gave her the look again. I got it just right so that it looked natural. They all looked at me. Then they burst out laughing, clutching each other. I don't think they were laughing at me. I'd have to do some more work on the look.

After that, I used to see her nearly every day. Now and then I'd catch her eye. I never spoke to her though. I thought she might laugh at me. Everything I thought of saying sounded really corny. I couldn't stop thinking about her. All day in school I'd be thinking, it won't be too long before I'm on the train, seeing her again. That train journey home was the highlight of my life. Then the bombshell burst. Mum said I'd have to start going to school on the bus because she couldn't afford the train fare any more, now Dad had left. I tried arguing with her. I explained it was really important that I travelled on the train because it gave me a chance to study and read books. But I couldn't get her to change her mind. I didn't say anything about Sheila Whiteley. I never told anybody about Sheila Whiteley. After that, the only time I'd get to see her was when the bus stopped outside the Catholic school and she was playing volleyball or tennis or something. I'd looked up her name in the phone book. I couldn't help reading her address over and over again. I'd even walked past her house. If she'd come out I was going to say, 'D'you know what number Danny Birkett lives at?' Danny Birkett trained the County under-fourteens football team. I thought she'd be impressed by that. For about half an hour I kept walking round the corner as if I'd just arrived and was in a terrible hurry. But she never came out. Then a lady with a dog came out of one of the houses and told me that if I didn't stop loitering she'd call the police. Later on I found she didn't live in that street after all. It was

47

somebody else called Whiteley. And now here she was in *my* street. She got off her bike and stood looking at the numbers of the houses. She had some envelopes in her hand. I had to speak to her this time. Even if I made a fool of myself I was going to speak to her. But I just couldn't hang about waiting. I had to be doing something. Cut the hedge. I'd be cutting the hedge, then just as she went past I'd turn round with a really surprised look on my face. 'Oh hello, haven't I seen you on the train . . .?'

I went to get the shears. Mum was laying tea out in the garden. It was Jo's birthday.

'I'm just going to cut the front hedge, Mum?'

Mum looked up in surprise. 'But you only did it yesterday.'

It was true. I hadn't cut the hedge for two years and now I was doing it twice in two days. I didn't have time to explain.

'Don't get too dirty. Uncle Edgar will be along soon.' I waved and rushed round to the front. I wouldn't start clipping straight away. That would be too obvious. I clipped a few stray branches of hawthorn and stepped back to admire my handiwork as though hedge-clipping was a work of art. A car drew up. I hoped it wasn't going to obscure my view.

'That's a good lad. Helping your mother out.'

Uncle Edgar and Auntie Edith climbed out of the car. Billy Fa Fa was bringing up the rear. The whole tribe. Auntie Edith was clutching a bunch of flowers.

'You're making a good job of that,' she said. I could see Sheila Whiteley getting nearer. I didn't want them around when I talked to her.

'Well I can't stop here talking all day,' said Auntie Edith. She and Uncle Edgar walked away towards the back garden. Billy Fa Fa stayed behind. I carried on clipping and pretended he wasn't there. But he wouldn't go away. Just stood there with his hands in his pockets watching.

'My dad's power cutter would finish that off in about five minutes,' he said. 'Oh yeah,' I said. I wasn't interested in his dad's power cutter. I just wanted him out of the way. There was a silence. I looked at him.

'You still there, Fa Fa?'

'You showed your Mum your report yet?' he asked.

I'd forgotten all about it. It was the worst report I'd ever had. On one exam paper I hadn't been able to answer a single question. I'd felt stupid handing in a blank piece of paper so I'd written Mr Morris, our history teacher, a letter telling him what it felt like to be looking at a paper where you couldn't think of anything to write. I was dreading Mum reading it. The brown envelope was still in my right hand pocket. I was putting off handing it over to Mum as long as possible.

'Bad one is it?' he said smiling.

I clicked the shears at him. 'How d'you fancy only having one ear?'

'Don't take it out on me just because you failed.'

'Who said I failed?'

He smiled. 'What you get for maths then?'

I hadn't expected him to ask for marks. I tried to think of a figure that wouldn't be unbelievable but would be good enough to surprise him.

'Sixty-five,' I said.

His mouth dropped open. 'Sixty-five!' he gasped. 'You lie in your rotten teeth, Langton.'

'Suit yourself,' I said dead casually. Why didn't he push off?

He went through all the subjects. I started getting carried away. My marks got better and better. By the end I'd given myself eighty-three for history. Fa Fa wasn't sure whether I was lying or not. As usual he managed to get in the last remark.

'Well your mother will be pleased won't she? Pity your dad won't be here to hear about it but then he's always too busy running off somewhere. Pity.' Then he walked off.

'Shut up, Fa Fa. At least he doesn't sell nappies like your dad.' It wasn't much but it was the best I could think of on the spur of the moment. Fa Fa just waved his hand and didn't look back.

I looked up the street. It was deserted. She'd gone. I'd missed my chance and it was all because of Billy bloody Fa Fa. I was really wild. I swore and thumped the hedge with my fist. Then I screamed in agony. I'd forgotten how sharp the thorns were. I tried to inch my hand out. The thorns were digging into my hand and wrist. I thought I was going to faint with the pain. There was blood trickling down my sleeve. Billy Fa Fa had a lot to answer for. I swore again, only louder this time.

'D'you know where Helen Darby lives?'

I looked round. Sheila Whiteley was standing right behind me. She had a piece of paper in her hand. I couldn't believe it. My throat went dry and I felt my face going red. 'Oh hello,' I said. I didn't need to act surprised. The words came out as though I had a throatful of porridge. I cleared my throat.

'I've seen you before, haven't I?' I tried to look as though it was very difficult remembering where it had been. She smiled at me. She had terrific teeth.

'Why have you got your hand in a hedge?'

50

It was a good question. I tried to pull it out but it hurt too much. I gasped in pain. I wondered if Sheila Whiteley would ever fall in love with someone who only had one hand. I tried to think of a reason for having my hand in a hedge. It wasn't easy.

'I didn't know you lived in our street.'

Of course I knew she didn't really. It was just a way of starting a conversation.

'You know I don't,' she said. She could see right through me. She was smiling though. I smiled back to show we were on the same wavelength. The blood was beginning to drip off my wrist on to the pavement. I eased it back into the hedge so that she wouldn't see. I winced.

'I'm looking for Helen Darby,' she said. 'I'm selling tickets for a Barn Dance so that we can build a new pavilion at the tennis club.'

The film started. I could see Sheila Whiteley in a short, white tennis skirt. She came over to where I was sitting on a bale of hay and asked me to dance. Over the stump of my right hand was a white bandage.

'Don't you know where she lives?'

I knew Helen Darby. She was a round-faced girl who wore glasses and had three brothers. I couldn't imagine her playing tennis.

'She lives at 37.' I tried to point but I had to swing nearly right round and keep my right hand in the hedge. 'It's tricky. Down that little drive.'

'Perhaps you could show me.'

What a chance! I couldn't believe my bad luck.

'I would,' I said, 'only . . .' I nodded at the hedge. 'I have to stay here,' I ended lamely. I tried to change the subject. 'I didn't see you coming.'

'Oh yes you did,' she said with another smile. 'You saw

51

me miles away then you ran off and came back and started cutting the hedge.'

I smiled back. My wrist was starting to go numb. I wondered if I was going to faint.

'You haven't told me why you've got your hand in the hedge.'

'It was a bird.' What had I said that for? I had to keep going. 'Yes, a bird. It flew in here. Dived.' I made a diving motion with my free hand and whistled. 'It broke its wing.'

'Oh, she said raising her eyebrows. She had terrific eyebrows. 'What kind of bird was it?'

I didn't know any birds. 'Robin.' I said. I wondered if *anybody* could go to the dance. Perhaps I could take up tennis.

'Can I help?'

'No, no. You have to keep calm. Hold it very gently.' This robin was becoming very real to me. 'When it calms down I can . . .' I didn't know what I could do. 'I can make it better.' I smiled weakly.

She swung her hair off her forehead. She had great hair.

'Well I have to be off.' She wheeled her bike off the pavement. I swivelled my head round, nodding in the direction of Helen Darby's.

'Just up the path,' I said.

She nodded. I had to say something.

'This dance,' I said. 'Can anyone go?'

'Of course. The more the merrier.' She rode off down the street looking back over her shoulder to shout, 'Maybe I'll see you there. That is if you can get out of the hedge in time.'

While she was still in ear-shot I kept talking to the robin telling him not to get excited. Then as slowly as I could I eased my hand out of the hedge. It was covered in blood and scratches. I wiped it on my trousers. I didn't notice the pain. I was thinking to myself. I've got a date with Sheila Whiteley. Well, it was a date in a way. She'd said she might see me there. That was as good as asking. There'd be about three hundred other people there; but it was still a date.

I'd never had a date before.

Chapter 5

I heard Mum calling me from the back garden. They were all sitting round a low table filled with sandwiches, lemonade and jellies. In front of Jo was a cake with six candles. I put my injured hand in my pocket and sat down.

'That's right, sit down old chap,' said Uncle Edgar. He was trying extra hard to be friendly. He offered me a chicken sandwich. 'Eat up. You could do with putting some skin on your bones.'

I took the sandwich with my left hand. What had my skin got to do with him?

'What do you say?' said Auntie Edith.

I mumbled thank you. Why did we have to have them round for Jo's birthday. It would have been better with just the three of us.

'Hands out of pockets,' said Auntie Edith. I carried on eating. She glanced at Uncle Edgar, frowning. There was a silence.

Uncle Edgar said in his quiet voice, 'Did you hear what Auntie Edith said?'

Out of the corner of my eye I could see Billy Fa Fa smirking. He was enjoying all this.

'Take your hand out of your pocket, Louie. There's a good boy.' Mum said. If Uncle Edgar hadn't been there she wouldn't have bothered.

'You don't need two hands to eat a sandwich,' I said. Jo was munching away but her eyes were going backwards and forwards following everything that was going on.

'Do what your mother says,' said Uncle Edgar. I kept my hand in my pocket and looked over towards Mrs Delaney's as if something very interesting was going on.

'Are you hiding something?' my mum asked.

'Can't I just eat my tea in peace?'

Uncle Edgar clicked his tongue. He looked at me severely over the top of his spectacles. 'Don't you speak to your mother like that.'

'I wasn't speaking to her like that.'

'And don't argue.'

'I wasn't arguing.'

'You were arguing.'

'I wasn't arguing, I was just explaining.' I had a sudden vision of Dad bursting through the back door and knocking Uncle Edgar flying into the flowerbeds.

'It doesn't matter, Edgar. I'm sure Louie didn't mean to be rude.'

'It does matter, Kate. I won't have him talking to you in that way.'

'The idea!' said Auntie Edith.

I put the sandwich down and pushed the plate away. I wasn't hungry any more.

Uncle Edgar hadn't given up yet. 'You haven't answered your mother's question.'

'What question?'

'Why are you hiding your hand?'

'I'm not hiding my hand.'

'Let me see it then.'

'What for?'

'Never mind what for. Let me see your hand.' He was getting really angry. I jerked my hand out of my pocket. The brown envelope containing my report dropped on the grass. But fortunately nobody noticed. Gently, I pushed it under the table with my foot. Mum gasped.

'Louie, how did you do that?'

'There, what did I say,' Uncle Edgar looked almost pleased.

'Go in and wash that hand straight away.' Auntie Edith thought you could die from having dirty hands at the table. Jo was looking at the blood on my wrist with interest.

'Pretty colour,' she said.

'Your mother's asking you how you did it,' said Uncle Edgar. 'Don't you think she deserves an explanation?'

I shrugged. 'I don't know.'

'Don't know!' said Uncle Edgar. 'How could you damage your hand like that and not know?'

'What's it got to do with you anyway?' I said.

'Louie!' said Mum.

'Well I never,' said Auntie Edith.

'Don't you dare speak to me like that, young man.'

I stared straight at him. 'Why, how should I speak to you?' We stared at one another across the table. Auntie Edith was flustered. She got up. 'You need some iodine on that hand.' She bustled towards the house. Jo was watching, her eyes wide open, clutching a glass of lemonade with both hands. Mum leaned forwards and put her hand on my arm. 'You mustn't talk to Uncle Edgar like that,' she said.

'Why not,' I said. 'What's it got to do with him anyway?'

'Louie, please!' Mum was trying to calm things down. 'Let's forget about it and eat our tea.' She smiled at Jo. 'Isn't this a lovely tea pot. Auntie Edith gave it to us.'

Uncle Edgar shook his head. 'I'm sorry, Kate. This has to be sorted out. He's got to learn that he can't talk to people like that. My goodness me, if I'd talked to my father the way you talked to me, Louie, I'd soon have known all about it.'

'Yes, but you're not my father, are you?'

'No, I'm not. Unfortunately your father doesn't seem to be very aware of his responsibilities.' Mum tried to say something but Uncle Edgar cut her off. 'No I'm sorry, Kate, this has to be said. I've felt this resentment building up for a long time. And from Jo as well. And it's got to stop. He's got to learn his manners somewhere. And if his own father isn't here to teach him some common courtesy well I suppose it's my responsibility. It's for your own good, Louie, believe me. You may not like it very much now but one day you'll look back and thank me for what I've done.'

Auntie Edith knelt beside me. She poured some iodine on to a ball of cotton wool and dabbed it on to my hand. I snatched it away.

'Leave me alone,' I shouted. The iodine spilled over Auntie Edith's lap. She leaped to her feet.

I thought Uncle Edgar was going to hit me. His head began to shake ferociously.

'Louie,' said my mum. She was nearly in tears. Jo began to cry.

'I'm covered in iodine,' said Auntie Edith.

'You really should go and wash your hands,' said Mum.

'What do I want to wash my hands for? She's just drowned them in bleeding iodine.' As soon as I'd spoken I was sorry. I hadn't meant to shout at Mum. It just came out.

Uncle Edgar was furious. 'How dare you swear at your mother,' he said. 'How dare you speak about my sister like that. After all she's done for you.'

He took a deep breath to calm himself down and then said quietly. 'Now, I want you to apologize to your mother.'

He stared at me and I stared right back.

Mum put her hand on mine. 'Just say you're sorry to me.'

I snatched my hand away and turned my head.

'Louie, just to me,' she said.

I looked at her. She looked really upset. She raised her eyebrows as though appealing. Everybody looked at me and waited. I looked straight at Uncle Edgar and said, 'I'm sorry, Mum.' I wasn't going to apologize to him. As soon as I'd said I was sorry, everybody tried hard to be nice to show it was forgotten. Then we ate in silence. Auntie Edith still looked upset though. She smelled like a hospital. She put on her bright smile. 'Didn't I see you speaking to a young lady a moment ago.' She must have eyes in the back of her head.

'What young lady?'

'You must know, dear. By the gate.'

'A young lady, eh?' said Uncle Edgar.

'Have you got a girl friend?' asked Mum. She was trying to turn it all into a joke. But I wasn't in the mood for jokes.

'She was just a girl, that's all.'

'Do we know this girl?' said Auntie Edith.

I sighed. 'I don't know. I've never seen her before.'

'D'you mean you picked her up?' The way Auntie Edith said it, it sounded like a disease.

'I'm sure she was a very nice girl,' said Mum.

'Oh I'm sure she was,' said Uncle Edgar, 'but we don't know that, do we?'

I sighed. 'Look, she's a girl from the tennis club. She

wanted to know where somebody lived. I told her. That's all. What was I supposed to do? Ignore her?'

Auntie Edith smiled. 'You were out there quite a long time dear.'

'We're only young once,' said Mum.

Uncle Edgar folded his fingers together and frowned. 'I don't think it's something we want to encourage. It doesn't do to have girls hanging round the front gate. Makes a bad impression.'

The way he was talking you'd think half the female population of Britain was trying to break down the front gate every night.

'What girls? She was one girl. That's all, one girl. I've never spoken to her before. She asked me the way and I told her. That's all.'

'I'm sure there's no need to raise your voice,' said Auntie Edith. 'We're only taking an interest in what you do.'

'I wasn't raising my voice. Why is it whenever I try to explain something I get told off?' I pushed away the cake I was eating. Jo wrinkled her brow. She didn't like arguments. She rocked slowly backwards and forwards. I thought, great birthday party she's having.

Auntie Edith coughed. 'Billy, pick up the iodine, there's a dear.' Fa Fa knelt beside me. I thought of stepping on his hand, but decided against it. I was in enough trouble as it was. When he came up he had this smirk on his face. Then I saw why. In his right hand was my school report.

'I found this on the ground,' he said, innocently. He laid the envelope on the table so that the writing was towards Uncle Edgar. It said *Louie Langton 3B. School Report.*

'I don't what it is,' Fa Fa said, as he sat down. He knew very well what it was. I could feel everybody's eyes on that envelope. Mum could see trouble coming. 'The geraniums are coming along nicely,' she said. Nobody answered. Everybody was looking at the envelope.

Uncle Edgar took out his cigarette case. He patted his pockets.

'Jo dear, be a good girl and get my matches. They're in my raincoat pocket.'

Jo stomped off up the garden. Uncle Edgar laid his unlit cigarette on the tablecloth and adjusted it until it lay straight. He cleared his throat.

'Billy had a very satisfactory report this term. Very satisfactory.' He took off his spectacles and gazed through them at the sky. Very deliberately he polished the lenses. Billy Fa Fa smirked.

'The Headmaster was very pleased with him,' said Auntie Edith.

I played with some crumbs on the table. Rolling them together into little balls. Mum was watching me. I stared at the brown envelope on the table.

'Sixty-three per cent for maths.'

Fa Fa smirked even more.

'Seventy-one for science,' went on Uncle Edgar. He eyed the envelope. 'How did you get on, Louie?' I kept on playing with the crumbs and said nothing.

'Well?'

'I did all right,' I said.

'Only all right,' Uncle Edgar shot a look at Mum. 'Perhaps we ought to have a look.'

'Look?'

'At your report.'

'It's not for you.'

'Louie!' said Mum.

'Well it's not.'

'He's perfectly right,' said Uncle Edgar. 'Strictly speaking, the report is not for me. It's for your mother. And your father of course. But I'm sure your mother would value my opinion.' Uncle Edgar spread his fingers and inspected his nails carefully. 'You see Louie, at this crucial stage in your school career, I might be able to give you some very valuable advice.'

Mum was looking at me. I frowned at her. I was trying to tell her that I didn't want anybody but her to read the report.

She said, 'Perhaps it would be better if we left it 'till after the birthday party.' She looked round. 'It's time to blow out the candles. Where is Jo with those matches?'

Uncle Edgar nodded. 'On the other hand,' he said 'if Louie were to let me look at it of his own free will it would be a sign of goodwill, of co-operation.' He smiled at me and reached across the table for the envelope. I snatched it from him. It wasn't his business. I was really angry. His pale shiny face seemed to fill all the space. I felt as though everything was crowding in and crushing me.

'What the bloody hell's it got to do with you? You're not my Dad.'

'No I'm not. And if I were, things would be very different.'

'Well you're not, so just keep your nose out or I'll . . .' I couldn't think how to finish my sentence. I was too angry. I stood up and swept half the crockery on to the floor. The teapot spilled over Auntie Edith. She screamed and stood up, trying to wipe the hot tea off her dress. I stormed away up the garden towards the house.

'Louie, Louie,' shouted Mum.

Uncle Edgar was striding after me. I slammed the kitchen door as hard as I could behind me. The glass cracked and shattered on to the floor. I looked back to see Uncle

61

Edgar's surprised face staring through the jagged edges of glass. I looked round. I didn't know where to go. I just wanted to escape. I wondered why Mum had lit a fire when the weather was so hot. There was a terrible smell of burning. I looked up. Clouds of black smoke were pouring across the upstairs landing and down the stairs. I turned back towards the garden, but Mum was already there.

'Harold! Harold!' she screamed. 'Come quick.'

'Water!' shouted Uncle Edgar. 'Fill anything you can find with water. And get some blankets.' Mum had disappeared into the smoke. I could hear her coughing and screaming for Jo. I filled a bucket and the washing up bowl with water, and rushed towards the stairs. Auntie Edith was ringing for the fire brigade. The smoke was coming out of Jo's room. Uncle Edgar came out coughing, his eyes red and running with water.

'It's Jo's bed,' he said as he snatched the water from me. I heard the water crashing. The smoke became thicker. Mum was sobbing for Jo. She tried to go into her room, but Uncle Edgar held her back. Auntie Edith brought blankets soaked in water. Uncle Edgar draped them over his head and plunged into the smoke once more. Gradually the smoke thinned out. Mum went into the bedroom. I heard her opening the windows. It can't have been too much of a fire because the flames were soon out. Jo's bed was black and smouldering in the middle. The blankets were badly charred. Mum kept saying, 'Jo, Jo,' over and over again. Uncle Edgar said, 'It was mainly smoke. But smoke can be more dangerous than flames.'

We'd caught it just in time. The smell was terrible and there was water and ashes all over the floor. Up the wall was a dark brown stain. But there was no sign of Jo. At first Mum was relieved because she hadn't been suffocated or burned. There weren't many places to look. Mum began to cry again. Suddenly she rushed to the window and looked down. She was frightened Jo might have jumped out. There were a lot of people in the street, all looking up. Mum shouted that the fire was out but that she couldn't find Jo. I went into my bedroom to see if she was hiding. It was empty. The bell of the fire engine rang down the street. Then I thought of something. I went into Mum's room and slowly opened the wardrobe door. I pulled Mum's fur coat aside. A pair of big eyes stared up at me.

'Mum! Mum!' I shouted. Mum pulled Jo out of the wardrobe and hugged her. She was laughing and crying all at the same time.

That night they made a little bed for her in my room.

I awoke in the darkness.

'Jo, Jo are you awake?'

She didn't answer but I heard her turning over.

'Jo,' I said, 'did you start the fire?'

'Yes,' she said. 'Weren't the flames pretty. It made me cough.'

'Jo. It was very bad of you,' I said. 'You could have burnt the whole house down. You could have been burned to death.'

It was strange trying to tell somebody off in the dark. I was frowning but of course Jo couldn't see me. I could hear her giggling.

'It wouldn't be funny if you'd burned the whole house down, would it?'

'Don't like this house. Don't like it any more.'

'How did it happen? Was it an accident?'

'It dropped.'

'What dropped?'

'Cigarette dropped.'

'Cigarette?'

'Dropped on the sheets.'

'You were smoking?'

'Yes, smoking. I like smoking.'

'You're not supposed to smoke. You're only five.'

'Six.'

'How long have you been smoking?'

'Don't know.'

'Where did you get the cigarettes from?'

'Uncle Edgar. I don't like Uncle Edgar.'

'God!' I let out a breath. Things were getting out of hand. What was happening to everything and everybody? It frightened me.

'Jo,' I said, 'You mustn't smoke.'

'I like them. I like the smell they make.'

I looked across the room towards her bed. There was a small pin point of red. It glowed larger and I heard Jo breathing out. Then it went in a small circle, stopped and circled back in the opposite direction. I climbed out of bed and switched on the light. Jo was sitting up in bed blinking. She held a cigarette in her hand. She was turning it in a slow circle. I snatched if from her and threw it out of the window. I sat on the edge of her bed and gripped her by the wrists. I made her look at me.

'Where were you hiding that cigarette?'

'Under the sheets,' she said.

'Jo, you must promise me never to smoke again.'

She stared up at me.

'Promise.'

64

'Promise,' she said.

'Cross my heart and hope to die.'

'Yes,' she said.

'Do it,' I said.

'Cross my heart and hope to die.'

I let go of her wrists and looked at her. 'Good. Now give me the matches.'

She dug down into the bedclothes and emerged with the box. She handed them to me. I turned towards the light switch.

'What about these?' she said.

She was holding up a packet of twenty cigarettes. I took them from her.

'Where did you get these from?'

'Uncle Edgar.'

'Where?'

'His raincoat.'

'These are going down the toilet,' I said.

I walked out on to the landing. The light was still on downstairs in the living room. Uncle Edgar's raincoat was hanging over the banister. I could slip them back. He wouldn't be any the wiser. I tiptoed down the stairs. It felt funny touching Uncle Edgar's raincoat. It made me shiver. I heard his voice and dodged back into the shadows. He was in the living room. I heard his voice say, 'Yes, but they need someone here all the time. They don't want a here-today-gone-tomorrow father.'

The door was slightly open. I crept closer.

'Yes I know that.' It was Mum's voice.

'Look at what happened tonight. Don't tell me that's got nothing to do with him being away. This is where a real father should be. Here. At your side, supporting you.

Being there when you need him. Not gallivanting about the place trying to relive his past.'

'I won't hear you say anything against him.'

'I don't know how you can defend him like you do. You know what got into him, don't you? He saw that fortieth birthday coming up and it frightened him. He could see his youth disappearing for ever. Dammit, the man's still a schoolboy. He's just never learned to grow up.'

'But I married him because of what he was. I knew what he was like. I can't blame him because he didn't become someone else. He tried, you know. He really tried. But it wasn't in him. Even when he's eighty I know that look will come into his eyes and he'll be off again.'

'Well, you know what I think. We've spoken about it enough. I know Joyce would have approved. God bless her.'

'I know Edgar, but he may come back.'

'Come back. How long is it this time? You don't even know where he is.'

'I don't know, six months.'

'Well if you need a steady father for those children you know you don't have to look far.'

'I know Edgar, I know.'

'Have you thought about it? I deserve an answer.'

I peeped through the crack in the door. Mum was leaning back on the sofa. She had taken her shoes off. Uncle Edgar was sitting in the armchair at her side. He was holding her hand in both of his. I put my hand up to my mouth. I felt sick.

Uncle Edgar leaned forward. 'But you'll think about it. Promise me you'll think about it.'

'I'll think about it.'

'I know you're worried about the children. But you'll

see, once they've learned to accept me as a father, things will be different.'

A rod of ice shot through my heart. Uncle Edgar was asking Mum to marry him.

Mum stood up and walked towards the door. She was close to me. I could have touched her. 'You have to give me time to think,' she said.

My head was reeling. I almost fell.

'Time,' said Uncle Edgar. 'How long?'

Mum ran her hand through her hair. 'I don't know. Three weeks. Give me three weeks.'

'I'll hold you to that,' said Uncle Edgar. He got up. 'I could do with a cigarette.' He walked towards the door. By the time he reached it I was back in my bedroom. My heart was thumping. I leaned on the bedroom door. I heard the front door closing and Uncle Edgar's car starting and driving away. I heard Mum putting out the lights and then going to the bathroom. She went to her bedroom. I wanted to go to her. To plead with her. Then it was quiet. I was alone in the dark. I thought about the fire. I remembered something. Something Mum had said during the fire. In all the excitement I hadn't realized. When Mum had shouted for help, she hadn't shouted for Uncle Edgar. She'd shouted 'Harold'. She'd shouted Dad's name. I thought she should have shouted louder: if she'd wanted Dad to hear she should have shouted louder all her life. But if he couldn't hear her calling then somebody had to go and fetch him. I knew who that somebody was. I got into bed. I was frightened. It really frightened me because this time, no matter what happened, I was going after him. I heard Jo's steady breathing. There was nobody I could tell. I pulled back the curtain. The moon came up above the window sill; white and completely round. It had been there that other night.

In some other place, that I'd have to find, Dad was under it.

I fell asleep and didn't dream.

Chapter 6

The guard was coming round again, checking the tickets. I slipped out of my seat and crept down the train. A red-faced man came out of the toilet doing up his belt. He had a can of beer in one hand. I stepped inside and closed the door behind, slipping the catch to 'ENGAGED'. There was water and paper all over the floor and someone had written Karen = Ricky in felt tip on the wall. I wondered who Karen was. Whoever she was I bet she was safe home in bed. I pulled down the seat and sat down. A train rattled by going the other way. Squares of light flashed past the window. Yellow light. Mostly though they were dark. Nearly everybody would be trying to sleep. I thought about all those people on the other train. They were all right. Leaning back asleep with their mouths open, asleep and contented. They knew where they were going. They had homes waiting for them. They'd walk up the paths to their front doors and ring their front door bells and some-one would open them and be pleased to see them. I didn't know where I was going. I wasn't even sure that Dad would be there. And if he was, whether he'd be pleased to see me. I felt in my pocket and took out the newspaper cutting. I read it for the twentieth time. I'd cut it out of Uncle Edgar's Sunday paper three weeks ago. It said:

LEGENDARY COUNTRY SINGER-SONGWRITER IN UK TOUR

Sunflower Management announce a nationwide UK tour taking in eight cities by American star, Murray Palermo.

Palermo will be bringing his own band with him and, apart from the concert tour, plans to record a new album during his visit.

'I love Britain and it's always been my ambition to record here,' the forty-year-old, Virginian-born singer announced. Palermo's last album achieved cross-over success and stayed thirty weeks in the Stateside 'Billboard' charts although it had less success over here. 'We aim to change all that through this tour,' said the six foot, smiling, bearded Virginian.

Then came a list of towns and cities. I'd ringed the one nearest to our town:

'The Town Hall, Birmingham, 8.00 p.m. July 19th.' That was tomorrow's date. I looked at my watch. Three a.m. No, tonight.

I hadn't told anybody except Jo that I was going off to look for Dad. I waited an hour after I'd heard Mum go to bed, quietly got dressed and crept into Jo's bedroom. Her action man was on the pillow. I shook her gently. She woke up straight away.

'Listen,' I said. 'I'm going to look for Dad. I think I know where he is. I'm not sure how long I'll be gone but tell Mum I'll ring every day so that she'll know I'm all right.'

'Where you going?' asked Jo.

I'd thought about that. 'I'm not telling you.'

'Why not?'

'Because Uncle Edgar and Mum will ask you where I've gone and if you don't know you won't be able to tell them.'

She looked round the room. 'All right, I'm coming.' She started to get out of bed.

'You can't come.'

'Why?'

'Because you've got to stay here and look after Mum. What d'you think she'd do if we both went? She wouldn't have anybody.'

'I want to come,' she said loudly.

'Ssh, you'll wake Mum up.' I gave her a white envelope. 'Give this to Mum tomorrow. It explains everything.'

'Want to come.'

'No. You can't. Look I'll bring you something when I get back.'

'Will you bring me chocolates?'

'Yes.'

She lay back on the pillow. I waited. Her eyes closed.

I went to the bathroom and picked up my toothbrush. I didn't bother with soap. I don't mind being dirty for a few days but I can't stand my teeth being furry. I took Mum's new toothpaste and went back into my bedroom to pick up my sports bag. When I came out Jo was standing at the top of the stairs, dressed in her duffle coat, wellingtons and sou'wester.

'Look,' I said as firmly as I could, 'I've told you you're not coming.'

'Why not?'

'I've explained that. Now go back to bed.'

I went downstairs. She was still watching me. I pointed at her bedroom and frowned.

I opened a tin in the kitchen and took out a fruit cake, cut off a slice and wrapped it in my shirt. Then I took a bigger slice. Then I decided to take the whole cake. Mum wouldn't mind. I threw a couple of oranges and three apples into the bag. Next to the cake tin was a small, hard-backed, notebook. I opened it. There was twenty pounds folded inside and a list of groceries and shopping. I took two fivers and wrote a little note. 'I've taken ten pounds. Only a loan. Will pay you back as soon as I get back.' Then I signed it and closed the book. I thought a bit and opened the book again; put back a fiver and wrote 'five pounds' instead of 'ten'. Thought again and added 'Dad' after where I'd put 'as soon as I get back.' I looked round for the last time. Mum had already laid out the cereal bowls and glasses for breakfast. I wouldn't be there.

Slowly I walked down the hall towards the front door. Jo was standing there dressed as she had been before only this time she had a small suitcase. I couldn't have her following me. Suppose I got to the bus stop and she jumped on. Or I suddenly looked round and there she'd be walking down the train corridor towards me. I'd have to bring her back. I'd never be able to get away again. I knelt down and looked her in the eyes. I had to pretend I was really angry. She was making it difficult for me to go. It doesn't take much to persuade you to go back to your nice warm bed when it's half past midnight and you're really not sure where you're going and it's dark and cold outside. Jo looked up at me. Her eyes were wide and staring.

'I don't want you with me. Can't you understand. You'd just be a nuisance. I don't want you round my neck all the time. Can't you get it into your stupid skull? I don't want you.'

She looked up at me, frowning.

'I don't want you. Clear off upstairs and leave me alone.'

She didn't cry. Just kept looking. Then she turned and walked slowly up the stairs. She still had her suitcase. She stopped and looked down at me.

'Wouldn't pester,' she said.

She was gone.

I felt as though I was in this film I'd seen where the father goes off to be shot by the gangsters that he's double-crossed. He's nearly in tears when he kisses his little daughter goodbye. 'Don't worry,' he tells her, 'Daddy will soon be back.' But he knows he won't. They look at one another for a long time and the little girl says, 'I know Daddy, I know.' The father hugs her and they both cry and you see him walking out into the streets as the music rises and the lights come on. All you could see was Kleenex. I felt really sad.

But it is one thing looking heroic in a film with thousands of people watching. It's different when it's just you. What happened if I fell under a train and nobody knew about it? I would just disappear from the face of the earth. Just sort of not be there any more. And who cared anyway? Only Mum and Dad and Jo. I wouldn't think Jo cared all that much after the way I'd just spoken to her. And if my Dad had really cared, why had he gone off like he did? Suddenly I felt tears coming into my eyes. I thought about how warm and cosy my bed would be. I went inside and sat down in the kitchen. I didn't think; I just sat there. I felt hungry. I opened the fridge. There was a leg of chicken in there. I was going to take a bite. Then I thought of the fire and Jo and Uncle Edgar. I slung the chicken into my bag and unlocked the back door. It was safer the back way, I kidded myself. I couldn't bolt it behind me. I left it open and crept down the garden, climbed over the fence at the bottom and into the lane. I put my foot in the rubbish. Something I couldn't see rustled away. I wondered if it was a dog. Or a rat? Or a fox? I shivered and turned my collar up. I looked back at the house. I'd left my bedroom and the bathroom light on. Mum would tell me off for that in the morning. Only I wouldn't be there to be told off. I wanted to see the house clearly for the last time. Fix it in my mind. An owl hooted.

I knew that an all night bus stopped by the roundabout on Culshaw Lane. I'd asked about the times two days before and I had the right money ready. I didn't want anybody asking me questions. A bus went by. There was hardly anybody on it. It was going the other way. There were two men at the bus stop. I hadn't expected there to be anyone else about. They weren't speaking. They must be going to work. Fancy having to go to work at half past midnight every day of your life. I realized these two would be waiting for this bus when I'd been asleep in bed. I hadn't known anything about them. Then I thought of all those other people lying in bed now who didn't know about me. I sat down on a low wall and yawned.

One of the men said, 'It's late this morning.' He had a sort of army haversack over his shoulders and big boots that were caked with cement and paint. The other man lit a cigarette and just grunted. I wondered if it might have been better to have walked further on, caught the bus half a mile from our house where there was less chance of being recognized. What I had to do was to look as normal as possible, to look as though travelling on a bus at half past midnight was what I did every day. If anybody asked me, I had a story ready. The school was going on a trip to France. We were meeting at the school in order to catch the coach. To make my story more believable, I'd brought my passport and a French phrase book with me. Standing there in the middle of the night waiting for the bus it didn't sound as convincing as it had yesterday morning.

The bus swung round the corner and squealed to a stop. The driver didn't even look at me. I went upstairs and sat

74

down trying to look at my phrase book. I wondered what the French for, 'I'm running away from home to find my father' was. They didn't have things like that. All they had was things like, 'The maid has brought me tea without sugar' and 'I have caught a cold from sitting in the draught please bring me the doctor/ambulance/ring the hospital/inform the British Consul/the local priest.' Going to France didn't sound too much fun.

I sneaked a look around. Mr Aretino! He was sitting right at the front with a cigarette in his mouth fast asleep. Mr Aretino was the husband of the lady who helped out at the cake shop where Mum worked on Saturday mornings. I watched out of the corner of my eye as the ash on his cigarette got longer and longer. I wondered how long it would get before it fell off. Would it burn his lips? Just before we got to the terminus at the station, the driver rang the bell. I pretended to be absorbed in my book. 'This room is too hot please give me another'. Mr Aretino got to his feet. The ash had fallen off and I hadn't seen it. I pretended to drop my book on the floor and ducked down out of sight after it. As I scrabbled on the floor amongst the cigarette butts I watched Mr Aretino walk past. His eyes were still closed.

The railway station was almost deserted. I waited in the shadows till nobody was about. One or two people came through. They walked straight on to the platform. They had season tickets. I felt like one of those prisoners they have in films who is trying to escape from Germany with a forged passport. Good job I could speak English. When there was nobody about I went to the ticket booth. The man behind the glass was reading last night's *Argus*. He didn't see me. I coughed. He carried on reading. I coughed louder. He looked up.

'Birmingham,' I said.

'What about it?' he said. He had those eyes where the top lids half cover the eyeballs.

I looked round. A porter was sweeping up dust and paper. I cleared my throat. 'I want a ticket there,' I said. The man just looked at me. He didn't believe me. I was going to be stopped and handed over to the police and I hadn't even got on the train.

'Birmingham,' I repeated. It sounded as if I was saying a password to someone who didn't share the secret.

'I heard you first time mate. What d'you want?'

'Ticket,' I said.

'Singreturn?'

'Pardon.' I was beginning to sweat.

He sighed. 'Are you coming back?'

'Oh yes. Well that depends, I think so.'

'Twenty-nine quid.'

'Twenty-nine?'

'Quid.'

There was a man behind me. I dropped my money on the floor.

'Twenty-nine quid. D'you want it or don't you? What you waiting for? You going to make me an offer?'

'How much is a single?'

'What you think?'

'Hurry up,' said the man behind me.

'Single, sixteen quid.'

If it had been Germany I'd be in the hands of the SS by now.

'I vill haf to ask my father for money,' I said. I wondered why I'd started speaking in a German accent.

'What?' said the man.

'I'll have to ask my Dad for more money.'

76

'You do that, sonny Jim,' said the man. 'Next.'

I walked away from the ticket kiosk. The man behind me was shaking his head. Sixteen quid! I'd thought it would be about five. I stood by the main gate. The train would be due any minute. Perhaps I could get a ticket to a stop before Birmingham and risk getting caught. But what would the man say if I went back and asked for another station? He was suspicious enough already. I felt everybody must be looking at me; just by looking they could tell I was somebody who was on the run. I pretended to read the timetables. A man came on to the station with a briefcase under his arm. He walked straight through the barrier and on to the platform. The porter who was sweeping didn't give him a second look. I looked round. He was looking at me. I nodded and smiled at him. He didn't smile back. He walked towards me. What had made him suspicious?

He said, 'What you fancy for the three thirty?'

'Nothing,' said a voice behind me. It was the ticket collector. He walked past me and stood beside the man with the broom. They both looked at his newspaper.

'Nothin'?' said the porter. 'He ain't running.'

The ticket collector laughed. While they had their heads in the paper, I slipped through and on to the platform. The train was just pulling in. I felt I'd lived a lifetime. What a story I'd have to tell them back at school.

BANG, BANG, BANG!

I woke with a start.

'Tickets please,' said a voice through the toilet door.

'Let's be having you. Tickets please.' I pulled the chain for something to do.

'You in there?' asked the voice.

'Yes,' I said. Of course I was in there.

77

'Come on out then.'

I couldn't think what to do. My heart pounded. I didn't seem to be able to move. There was more banging on the door.

'If you're not out in two seconds, I shall have to take further measures.'

I opened the door. The guard looked down at me from a great height.

'Got your ticket?' he said.

I went through my pockets as if searching for it.

'You have got a ticket haven't you?'

'No,' I said.

'You haven't?' The guard frowned. 'Don't you know it's a serious offence to travel without a ticket?'

I just looked up at him. I felt as if I was about five years old. I'd tell him the truth. Somebody I remembered had said once that honesty was the best policy. I wondered where to start. It was a long, long story. Start at the beginning.

'Well, my dad . . .'

'Oh your dad's got it, has he?'

I shifted tack swiftly.

'Yes,' I said, 'that's right, my dad's got it.'

The guard looked disgruntled. 'Oh blimey, where's he then?'

I needed time.

'Pardon?'

The guard sighed, 'Your dad, where is he?'

'He's on the train.'

'I know he's on the train,' said the guard looking at the ceiling. 'If you think I'm walking back up this train looking for your dad, you've got another think coming.'

'He's back there,' I said pointing. 'I had to go to the

78

toilet. They were all being used. I had to come right down to this one.'

'Without your ticket.'

'Without my ticket.' There was a silence. I was frightened he might ask me to fetch it and bring it back. I kept talking.

'He's taking me to meet my sister in Birmingham. We're going on a school trip. To France.' I reached into my bag. 'I've got a phrase book and my passport in here. There's some good phrases in case you need the doctor or anything.'

The guard pushed his cap back. 'Yeah well, I'm not too interested in French at the moment, it's your ticket that I want.' He sighed again. 'All right you go back to your Dad. And next time sonny, ask him to give you your ticket, then I won't have to walk my bleeding legs off.'

'I will,' I said. 'Thank you.'

'Merci buckups,' he said and shambled off down the corridor. He looked like a big bear.

I walked up the corridor as far as I could and found an empty compartment. It was beginning to get light. A milk cart came the other way on a parallel road. We went through a station but so fast I couldn't read the name. I pretended to sleep but the guard didn't come back.

An hour later the train began to slow. The brakes ground. I opened my eyes and saw grey buildings, factories, a row of houses and a church. The next danger would be going through the barrier. If they stopped me I'd say, 'My Dad's got my ticket,' and point at someone on the other side of the barrier. When I was through I'd just run. The film in my head wouldn't stop. I saw myself bumping into something big and blue. My head came up from a

79

large pair of boots. A policeman! I shook my head to rid myself of that disaster.

I got out with everybody else. A big sign said 'New Street.' I tried to lose myself in the crowd of people. We all went together up an escalator but we had to climb because it wasn't working. There was a large barrier at the top of the stairs with five or six turnstiles. Everybody was being asked to hand in their tickets. My heart stopped and I slowed down. The other passengers crowded past me. Two policemen stood at the barrier.

I thought, 'Mum must have told them. Jo had woken her up. She guessed where I was going and rang the police.' There were two other men beside the police. They were all looking towards me. I dawdled, hiding behind a fat man carrying two suitcases. One of the policemen shouted, 'There he is,' and pointed at me. I just stood still. The policemen and the two other men came at me and then went past. They had a stretcher. I looked behind. A porter was waving to them. 'Over here,' he was calling. Two ticket collectors were standing together looking down the station past me.

'Reckon he had a heart attack.'

'Yeah?'

'Crewe they reckon. Just left Crewe.'

I slipped through the empty turnstile and didn't look back. Every second I expected a shout. But none came. I just walked with the crowd. There were more people about now and I felt safer. The big round clock said seven o'clock. I walked out on to the street. There were large grey buildings everywhere and lots of waste paper blowing about. I asked a man in uniform where I could find the Town Hall. I went where he pointed down a long corridor that had shops on either side. Everybody seemed to know

80

where they were going. I didn't seem to be able to find the street.

At last I came out into daylight. Steps led up in different directions. None of them said 'Town Hall'. I went up the steps nearest to me. A stream of cars whizzed by. I crossed the road and wandered along gazing into shop windows. On the other side of the road it was quieter. I sat down on a wooden bench. An old woman with her coat tied around her waist with a piece of string began burrowing in the waste paper basket. She mumbled to herself. She asked me if I had any money for a cup of tea. When I said no, she swore at me and shuffled on. I looked in my bag; took out the chicken leg and began to eat it. Four black boys with green and gold baggy berets went by laughing. One carried a big cassette player. I could hear the music long after they'd disappeared.

I stood up, wiping my hands on my trousers. Two ladies came by. I asked them if they knew where the Town Hall was. They pointed up a street full of shops.

'Do I have to get a bus?' I asked.

'No, It's only about three hundred yards. Wouldn't you say, Alice?'

Her friend nodded.

I walked in the direction they pointed. Everywhere I went it seemed to be windy. Four girls went past talking and giggling. They wore blazers and ties. They were going to school. I wished I was going with them. For the first time in my life I wished I was going to school. I thought, I'm a fugitive, a fugitive from justice. I put on my look. It wasn't difficult because of the dust that was blowing in my eyes.

I thought if the girls came up and spoke to me I'd say, 'I can't tell you anything about my life. I'm a fugitive you see.' And they'd look impressed and worried for me and the prettiest one would fall in love with me. We'd just look at one another and know. 'You don't have to worry about me,' I'd say. 'It's just my life, my lonely life.' And I'd walk slowly out of sight. They'd look after me with sad but admiring looks until I was out of sight. Afterwards they'd talk about me and never forget.

'Here, mind where you're going,' shouted a man in a car and blared his horn.

I came to a patch of sloping grass with a bigger building of grey stone at the top. Next to it was a larger building with pillars. It looked like a Greek or Roman building. I knew that, because last year we'd built the Parthenon out of papier maché and plaster of Paris in R.E. with Mr Hallows.

Behind one of the stone pillars a lady was going through a small door with a bucket. I ran across the road.

'Excuse me,' I said. 'Is this the Town Hall?'

She put her bucket down and wiped her hand across her forehead. Another lady came out with a mop. 'Town Hall,' she said, 'ah, this is the Town Hall.'

'Not open yet,' said the other.

'I was looking for this man . . .' I started to say.

'Aren't we all?' said one. They both laughed and the laughter changed into coughing.

'He's playing here tonight. His name's Murray Palermo.'

They both looked at one another. 'Murray . . .?'

'Palermo.'

'Palermo, don't know about him.'

'Wasn't he cancelled, Dolly?'

'Cancelled?' I brought out my crumpled sheet of newspaper. 'It says here he's on tonight.'

They both bent over the newspaper.

'Aw that's him all right, isn't it Doll? He was cancelled.'

'That's out of date, your paper.'

I couldn't believe it. I thought of my bed at home. 'I've come miles,' I said.

'You could get your money back if you had a ticket,' said the one called Dolly.

'Definitely cancelled,' said the other. 'It says on the poster.'

'The box office'll be open in about three hours. Get your money back then.'

I didn't want my money back. I wanted to find my Dad.

'He's on in Southport tomorrow. You could see him there.' She pointed at my newspaper.

I took my paper cutting back. 'Thank you,' I said.

I put it in my pocket and walked round to the front of the building. There was a large poster on the wall with a list of names. A piece of paper had been glued across. On it was written 'Tonight's show Cancelled.' I could still read Murray Palermo's name faintly underneath.

I looked round. The two ladies had gone inside. There was no point in hanging about. But I had a feeling that if I stayed maybe the information would turn out to be wrong. But every poster I saw had CANCELLED written on it.

I felt like giving up and going home. Where was Southport? It sounded as if it was by the seaside somewhere. Perhaps it was in Cornwall. Wherever it was, it would be miles away.

I sat down on the Town Hall steps. Outside the Post Office a man was selling newspapers. His voice was cracked and broken with shouting. On a small hoarding in front of him was written: 'Parents' Agony over Murdered City Schoolboy.'

Streams of cars and trucks and buses roared round the

island. It was like being stranded in the middle of a noisy roundabout.

I remembered a line from a film Dad had taken me to see years ago. A cowboy walks into a saloon and asks the barman, 'What kind of town is this?'

'A good town to be leaving,' says the barman.

I got up and walked back the way I'd come.

Southport might be better.

Chapter 7

Five minutes after accepting the lift from him I knew I was in trouble. I knew how you had to be careful about getting into cars with strangers. Only last year there'd been that trouble at school when Dave Maddocks had disappeared. We'd been playing with him in the same park twenty minutes before he'd got in the car. The man told him that his mother had been taken to hospital and that he'd come to drive him there. He'd asked Noel Curry if he'd go with him too. But he'd said no. They'd found Dave Maddock's body five days later in the old air raid shelter by the canal.

But this bloke hadn't looked like that. You'd expect a pervert to be old and ugly with a long raincoat and thick glasses. The man in the car didn't look like that at all. He was young for a start and was wearing a suit. Anyway I was fed up with waiting for the Liverpool bus. Southport was only twenty miles from Liverpool. I'd decided to phone my Mum from a kiosk. I was in the middle of telling her I was all right, when the bus drew in. I said goodbye. She kept asking me where I was.

'I'm all right,' I kept saying. I had a feeling she was crying. I had a feeling if I carried on talking to her I might tell her where I was going to. I was quite glad when the coach pulled in because it gave me an excuse for saying goodbye.

But the coach was full. I followed the driver round as he was putting everybody's luggage in the back. Couldn't he squeeze me on? I didn't mind standing.

'There'll be another one along in three hours,' he said. 'Your best bet is to go to the bus station in Digbeth. It's only about a mile and a half from here. You've got more choice there. They'll tell you what to do.'

It had taken me an hour to find this bus stop. I didn't want to walk a mile and a half through Birmingham again.

The bus drew out. I sat down on a bench by the stop. Everywhere you went it seemed to be windy. Across the dual carriageway a priest came out of the church and walked along the pavement. His black robes whirled out behind him. An ambulance came out of the hospital behind me, its siren blaring and blue light flashing. Then the car drew up. The driver wound down the window. 'Going anywhere I'm going?'

I was so fed up I didn't think. 'Southport', I said.

'Hop in,' he said.

Just as I closed the door I had this strange feeling. I can't say what it was. It was a kind of warning. I almost got out of the car straight away; and then I thought how embarrassing it would be. I looked round. It was a big car.

'Just get my clobber out of your way.' He bent down and picked up a sports bag full of clothes. There was a pair of football boots and a hockey stick on the top. He slung it on the back seat. I thought, if he plays football he must be all right.

'I'm going to Liverpool. The 'Pool,' he said in a mock Liverpool accent and laughed. I smiled. 'You can easy get a lift from there.'

'Thanks,' I said.

'Not much fun waiting out there. Waiting long? By the way my name's Jim, what's yours?'

'Louie.'

'Louie,' he said as if he was surprised. 'That's an unusual

86

name. A very unusual name. I bet your Dad gave it to you.' He patted my knee and laughed. I didn't give a very good smile back.

He kept asking me questions and listening to me as if what I was saying was very important.

'How d'you get a name like Louie?' He said it in a funny way that made me feel embarrassed. I got fed up with explaining about my name. In fact my Dad *had* chosen it. He'd once met a trumpet player called Louis Armstrong and had told him if he had a son he'd name him after him. He did the same with Jo. She was called Jolene after Murray Palermo's sister but everybody called her Jo. I didn't want to tell Jim all that. I didn't like him touching my knee like he did.

'My Dad just liked it, that's all.'

'Good name. Good name,' said Jim. 'At least it's different. Anybody calls out Jim and twenty guys turn round. At least with Louie you know who they're talking to. Am I right? I'm right.' He laughed again.

He took a cigarette case out of his inside pocket and pressed the cigar lighter.

'Cigarette?' he asked, flicking the case open.

'No thanks,' I said.

He took a cigarette and lit it. 'Very wise,' he said.

There were initials stamped on the cigarette case. 'C.G.R.' Why did he have that on when his name was Jim?

'Wish I'd never started,' he said, 'specially if you do a bit of kicking the old ball about.'

I wish that there'd been someone with me. Even Billy Fa Fa.

'You play football at all, do you? I notice the sports bag.'

'I play a bit. For the School, under-fourteens.'

'I bet you do too. You've got the look of a footballer.

87

Good strong legs I bet.' He squeezed my leg again. I flinched away. He didn't seem to notice but carried on pressing. i started to get really frightened. He opened the window and blew smoke out. 'I bet you're an inside forward. Am I right? I'm right aren't I?'

'Goalkeeper,' I said.

'Ah,' he said, 'that makes sense. You've got the hands. Just look at the size of those hands.' He laid his left hand across on top of mine. 'Need big hands of course, if you're a goalkeeper. And agility of course. Bet you're pretty agile when you get between those sticks Louie.'

I took my hands away. He laughed.

'Don't like to be touched, do you?'

I thought of Dave Maddocks lying dead in the air raid shelter.

'Have to get used to the old physical contact. Football's a very physical contact game. Oh yes, the old phys con is the name of the game.'

He was turning off the motorway. Why was he turning off? I remembered the newspaper hoarding I'd read outside the Town Hall. 'Parent's Agony over Murdered City Schoolboy.'

My mouth had gone dry. We were driving down a country lane. I wondered if he went slowly enough round a corner I could throw myself out. But he looked strong and fit. He was looking at me and smiling. He ran his fingers through his hair.

'You got a girl friend, Louie?'

I thought of Sheila Whiteley. I didn't want to mention her name in his car. Didn't think it was right to think about her. 'No,' I said. As soon as I said it I knew I'd said the wrong thing.

'Don't blame you, Louie. Don't blame you. Too much

trouble, women. Take my advice, nothing but trouble. Better off without 'em.'

He had a suit in a cellophane hanger against my door post. As we swung past a pub and round a corner it tilted and struck me.

'That in your way, is it?' He leaned across and pushed it back then rested his hand on the back of my neck.

'You boys like to wear your hair short these days. Not like when I was a kid.' He tugged gently at the hair on the back of my neck. 'If you can believe it Louie, when I was your age I had it down over my shoulders. Right down over my shoulders. Fashion. That's all it was Louie. Fashion.' He pulled my hair sharply. I reached up and took his hand away. He laughed.

'You really are very touchy. Louie. You must learn not to be so touchy.'

My palms were sweating and my heart pounding.

'Here, you know what I reckon your problem is. You got knocked about when you was a kid. I'm right aren't I, Louie? I reckon,' he paused as he turned a corner looking left and right, 'I reckon you was one of those battered babies you read about. I think that's a shame Louie, I reckon that's a real shame because what that means is that you can't bear anybody touching you, after.'

I had to say something. The roads were becoming more and more deserted. 'Why have we come off the motorway?' I tried to say it as if I wasn't worried.

'Jimmy boy knows a short cut.' He glanced down at the instruments in front of him. 'Need a drop of the old gasolino, Louie.'

He tapped my knee again. 'I have an idea. My sister has a house near here. I sometimes stay there when I'm on business near Liverpool. Now she's away at the moment so what we could do, what we could do, Louie, is to stop over there tonight and then I can drive you to Southport tomorrow. How does that grab you?'

I could see myself lying in a field my arms spread-eagled; see my picture in black and white on the front page of a newspaper. I'd rather take the risk of throwing myself out on to the road and making a run for it. Keeping my eyes on the winding road in front I let my left hand slide down an inch at a time towards the door handle. I felt the cold metal beneath my fingers. Suddenly, as hard as I could, I pushed down and put my shoulder against it. It didn't give.

'Child lock,' said Jim smiling. 'Very handy. Stops kids falling out. Could have a very nasty accident. Kids falling out into the road as you're going along.' He suddenly put his foot on the accelerator and the bonnet of the car lifted under the roar of power. He smiled. 'Especially if you're going fast.' He suddenly slowed again. A small country service station lay in front of us.

'Ah, gasolino.'

He pulled up by the pumps.

'You stay there Louie boy while Jim fills her up.'

He got out, removed the hose from the pump and moved to the rear of the car. I knew there was a button in the door sill that you lifted if you wanted to unlock the door from the inside. I couldn't see it because it was behind my left shoulder. I looked in the rear view mirror. Jim was leaning over the petrol filler. He noticed me looking and smiled and winked at me. Very slowly I let my right hand creep across my body to the door and then upwards. I could hear him screwing the filler cap back on. Soon he'd be back. My fingers inched up the door until they reached the sill. Slowly, a millimetre at a time I felt behind me.

Where was it? I'd reached the window frame. I should have found the button by now. The driver's door opened.

'Not going anywhere are you?' he said.

I scratched at my left shoulder as if it was itching.

'Forgot the money,' he said. He reached into the glove compartment and took out a wallet. He winked at me again then closed the door and locked it. I looked behind me at the door. Where the button should have been was a hole. I glanced across to the driver's door. It was the same. Both buttons had been removed on purpose. That meant that Jim had planned this. That he'd done it before. There had been others before me. There was blood on my lip. I'd bitten it so hard that it was bleeding. In the rear view mirror I could see him walking towards the kiosk. A pick-up truck pulled in, towing behind it a high sided trailer. A boy of fifteen clambered out of the passenger door. I banged on the window and waved for him to come over. He smiled at me and walked past towards the kiosk. He thought I was being friendly. I wiped the blood off my lip with the back of my hand.

'Oh God,' I said out loud. It was funny how you only prayed when you were in trouble. Mum believed in God. I wondered if he was up there somewhere, watching me. I looked up. Light was coming through a crack in the roof. He'd left the sunroof slightly open. I looked round. I could see his back in the queue. I stood up and pressed with all my might on the sliding panel. It moved a few inches then stopped. I looked round. On the back seat was a hockey stick. I wedged it hard into the crack and jerked it back with all my strength. It slid a few more inches but still not wide enough for my body to get through. I glanced at the kiosk once more. He was talking to the girl at the till. I threw all my weight and strength on to the stick. There

91

was a sharp crack as it splintered. But the roof opening was wider. I pushed my bag through and clambered out on to the roof and out.

I could see Jim at the desk of the kiosk. He was saying goodbye and turning. I ran as fast as I could round the further side of the building. I pushed my back against the wall. I could see Jim's legs under the high-sided trailer. He was getting into his car. His feet left the ground. He'd soon be gone. I let my breath out in relief. Then I heard footsteps.

'Louie, Louie. I'm waiting for you.'

He was walking towards me. Any second he'd be round the side of the building. I edged along the wall, my back to it. I found a door. Another door. I turned the knob and fell into a small whitewashed room with a washbasin. At the back was a door with a foot of space at the top and the bottom. It was a toilet.

'Louie. Come on Louie.'

I pushed through the door and shot the latch. If he came in here there was nowhere else I could run to. I heard his footsteps stop outside. I could picture him looking this way and that.

'Louie that wasn't very nice. Scratching the roof of my motor. Not very nice at all. If you'd wanted to go Louie, you only had to tell me. I'd have understood. But now you owe me. D'you understand, Louie?'

I held my breath. I could hear the tap dripping.

'Louie.' There was silence.

Then I heard him bang the door open. Heard his footsteps on the concrete. Another door banged open. I expected to see his face staring at me. But it didn't.

I heard him swear. 'Bloody kid.' Funny how his voice sounded fainter though he was inside. Then the door closed and I heard his footsteps disappearing. He'd gone. I counted up to a thousand. And then another thousand for luck. I unlocked the cubicle and opened the outside door a crack. The pick-up and trailer was still there. I craned my neck to see round the corner of the building. The pumps were deserted. Jim had driven away. A lady walked towards me. She stopped and looked at me. What was up with her? I stepped out into the sunlight. 'Well I never!' she said and walked past me shutting the door. I looked at the closed door. It had 'Ladies' written on it. Jim hadn't thought to try that one. No wonder the lady had given me that funny look. I walked across towards the kiosk. My heart stopped. Jim's car was over by the fence. Jim was leaning over away from me putting air into the rear tyres. He hadn't seen me yet. I tried the door of the high-sided trailer. There was a lock on it but it wasn't padlocked. I unhooked it, opened the door and slipped inside pulling the door shut behind me. It was almost pitch dark in there. After the brightness of the sunlight I was blind. Something moved. There was a rustling and creaking sound. I wasn't alone in there. Somebody else was moving about.

'Hello', I said softly.

A huge dark bulk struck me. My head struck the wooden side of the trailer with a crack. I felt a slight sickness in my throat and then I was on the floor and the darkness became total.

Chapter 8

When I came to, it wasn't like it is in films where somebody gets punched and just shakes his head and is all right again. As soon as I opened my eyes I was sick and I went on being sick for about half an hour. I couldn't stand up if I'd wanted to. I remembered Jim right away. At first I thought he must have hit me and I was lying down in the back of his car but then I remembered going into the trailer and something hitting me. There was a snorting noise. I looked up.

A great triangular head bent in my direction. Two huge nostrils breathed hot breath all over me. I was in a horse box and I don't think the horse was particularly pleased to have me sharing his home. Luckily he was tied in pretty tight. He couldn't move very far, but it didn't leave much room for me. There was a strong smell of straw and muck. The horse box was rolling about quite a bit. I sat down in the straw and tried to be sick again. I wondered if I'd lost my memory. Like in that film *Going Back To Nowhere* where this man wakes up in a room with a gun in his hand and a dead man in a chair. He can't remember anything, not even his name. Dad was a reporter in a train in that one. Actually you only saw his legs going past as the man's hiding in this sleeping compartment. I wondered if I'd lost *my* memory. I felt my head where I'd banged it. There was no blood. Just a very big bump. I hadn't thought that being knocked out would hurt as much as that. I said to myself, 'My name is Louie Langton. I live at 39A Willow

Street. I'm looking for my Dad.' Everything seemed to be in order.

I'd never been as close to a horse as this before. When you see them racing on the telly they don't look that big. Close to though, he towered over me. He kept moving his back hoof and you could see big veins running all over his stomach. He had really long eyelashes. I hadn't noticed that horses had eyelashes before. The trailer went round a corner and I was thrown against the horse. I was really worried in case he started kicking. If he got mad there wouldn't be much hope for me. I was scared. The horse was eating some hay kind of stuff that was in a grating at the front. He didn't seem to be bothered now about me being there. I thought about those films where these young American boys find a horse that no one else can tame. There's always this one boy that the horse will trust. Nobody else can get near him except this one boy. There was a window at the front end. If I could get up there I could see where we were and who was driving. I inched my way up, talking to the horse. I knew I was supposed to sound confident. They were like dogs. They could smell if you were afraid and bite you. I thought about the boy in the film.

'Good boy.' I kept saying. 'There's a good boy. You don't want to bite Louie do you? You're a good boy, Louie's your friend.'

There was a terrible splashing, cascading torrent from the tail end. It seemed to go on for about five minutes. The horse just kept on eating. He was used to it, I suppose.

'Good girl,' I said soothingly, 'there's a good girl.' A cloud of steam was slowly rising. The smell was really strong. I hoped she'd missed my bag.

I looked through the window. There was a lady in a

headscarf driving and next to her was a thin-necked boy of about fifteen. There was no point calling to them or trying to attract their attention. Perhaps when we got to wherever they were going I'd have a chance to dodge out. Even if they caught me I could tell them about Jim. They'd understand. Why should they believe me though? It sounded like a made-up story. I could tell them about Dad. At least I could show them the piece of newspaper. The woman would probably want to phone my mother; then it would be all over. No, I'd have to make up a better story. It was funny that you had to make up a lie to get people to believe you. The horse was looking at me. I wondered what he was thinking. The pick-up pulled off on to a lane. I wondered if we were going to Southport. Perhaps that's where she lived. That would be good. The boy looked round to check that the horse was all right. I ducked down. The trailer bumped up and down over the track. I started to feel sick again. At last it manoeuvered backwards and forwards and stopped. The engine was switched off. I heard them slamming the car doors and then they were round the back. I picked up my bag and got ready to make a dash for it. There was straw and dirt all over my coat where I'd been rolling on the ground. The door rattled. I heard the padlock being taken off. I remembered that Greek story that Old Morris had told us in class about how these warriors get past the giant with one eye by hanging underneath a load of sheep. I decided not to try it with the horse. I crept to the back of the horse and stood flat against the wooden wall on the other side of the hinges. The door opened and a shaft of sunlight cut through. I held my breath. If the worst came to the worst I'd just run. Knock them over and keep running. They wouldn't be expecting anybody to be in there. I saw the boy's hand on the door.

'Just look at this tyre, Tony,' said the lady's voice. The boy's hand disappeared and I heard them walking to the front of the trailer. The car had been backed against the open door of a stable. I didn't think twice but dodged into the gloom. There was a stall for the horse against one wall and an archway at the back that led into a large barn. I slipped through the arch and threw myself behind three bales of straw. On my left was a large mound of loose straw with some pitchforks in it. A thin beam of light came from an opening up near the roof. I heard the rattle of the horse's hooves and then a different, hollower sound as they brought her into the stable and tied her up.

The lady in the headscarf said, 'Feed her, Tony, and give her a night rug.'

'You want her rubbing down, Miss?'

'No just quarter her.'

'Yes Miss.'

The lady walked away. The boy she'd called Tony picked up a bucket and took it outside. The loose mound of straw looked safer. I crept round the bales and dived into the straw covering myself as well as I could. I kept a small portion open. Enough for my eye to peep out and see what was going on. Outside I heard the boy shouting.

'You want me after that, Miss?'

'No,' I heard the lady calling further off, 'but I shall want you six o'clock tomorrow morning.'

The boy came back in. Put some feed in the rack and undid the cloth blanket at the front and began to brush down the horse's neck and shoulders, the chest and between the front legs. Then he put a heavier blanket over

97

the horse and tied it down. He whistled as he worked, speaking softly to the horse every now and then.

'There, my lady,' he'd say, 'just lift that leg. That's it my girl.' He seemed fond of the horse.

I was wondering if they locked the stables at night. She looked a valuable horse. If I was going to get away I'd have to do it before the boy locked up. On the other hand the straw was warm. The only thing was that it smelled really bad. I shifted to a cleaner place. It smelled bad there too. It must be me that smelled.

The boy came through into the barn. I ducked down and kept as still as I could. He picked up a pitchfork and came over to where I was lying. He lifted it up ready to plunge it in. There was nothing for it. I lifted the straw back. When he saw the straw move, he stepped back in amazement.

'My God, what is it?' he whispered.

There was a voice from the door. The lady said, 'I'm sorry Tony, I forgot. Could you have a look at the tyre. See if you can do something.' The boy held the pitchfork high and still. He stared down at me.

'Tony?' said the lady.

The boy kept staring down at me without blinking. Neither of us moved. We were like two statues. After what seemed an age Tony said, without taking his eyes of me, 'I'll have a look at it tonight, Miss.'

'Thank you.'

'Probably a slow puncture, Miss.'

'Yes, goodnight.'

He still had his eyes on me.

'Goodnight, Miss.'

He motioned with the pitchfork that I was to get up. I stood up slowly. Keeping the prongs of the fork pointed at me he pushed me into the light. We looked at each other for a long time. He was wearing a cloth cap like old men do and yellow trousers that were tucked into his socks and wellingtons. His hair was cut very short at the side and although he looked fifteen or sixteen he was much shorter than me.

'What you doing here?'

I licked my lips. 'I was hiding.'

'I can see you was hiding. What was you hiding from?'

'It was at that petrol station. I had to get away from the bloke.'

'Why?'

'He gave me a lift. He was trying to; he. . .'

'Funny geezer was he? How you get here then?'

'In the box.'

'What, our horse box? And she let you!'

'She knocked me over. I was unconscious.' I fingered the bump on my forehead.

'She give you that, did she?'

'It wasn't her fault,'

'I see.'

'Well I don't know,' he said, 'sounds fishy to me, know what I mean. You could be after the horse for all I know. What you got in your bag. You ain't got dope and little needles have you?'

'No.'

'That's what you say. Sling us your bag.'

I threw it to him. He picked it up. I thought he'd look inside it but he just emptied everything on to the floor. He could see there was only my clothes. All the food had gone.

'Ain't got nothing hidden on you?'

'No,' I said. The room suddenly was upside down. I was face down in the straw. He leant over me.

'Here, you all right?'

My head cleared. He sat down beside me.

'You don't half pong. It's that jacket. You smell worse than the horse.'

'I was at the wrong end.' I said.

He laughed. 'Story of my life. Always at the wrong end.'

He asked me where I'd come from and who I was. I told him the whole story. He told me he'd always wanted to be a jockey. Half way through he asked, 'Here you hungry?'

I suddenly realized I was. I thought, I must be feeling better.

'Look,' he said, 'You wait here. I'll see if I can get you something. And give us your jacket and your trousers. I'll let you have something of mine. All right?' I gave him my jacket and slipped off my trousers.

'Good job your fruity pal in the car ain't here, he wouldn't half fancy you.' I laughed. It felt funny sitting in the straw with no trousers on.

'You wait there. I won't be a tick.' He went out closing the door behind him.

I wasn't going far without my trousers. It suddenly struck me that he'd tricked me. He'd pretended to be friendly then got me to take off my trousers so I couldn't get away even if I'd wanted to. He'd come back with someone else and that would be the end of me. The door opened. He came in. I heard him whisper to someone in the darkness. I picked up the pitchfork. The shadow came towards me. It was Tony. He was on his own. He looked at the pitchfork in my hand.

'What we doing, playing at farmers, are we?'

100

I felt ashamed. 'I thought I heard you talking to someone.'

'The horses pal, the horses. That's what you end up doing round here. Look, here's a jacket.' He threw me a thick brown donkey jacket. On the back was written 'Deering Racing Stables'. And a pair of trousers. 'They're not mine. Mine would be too short. You put mine on they'd fetch up round your knees. You'd look like a boy scout. I nicked these off another lad. He won't miss 'em and if he does, you'll be miles away.'

I sat down and went to pull on the trousers.

'Here, I'd wash if I was you. Get the horse shit off.' He brought a bucket of water over. Unwrapped a towel. 'Got you some soap as well. Nothing but the best at this hotel.'

I took off my shoes and socks and washed as well as I could. While I did, Tony told me about his life as a jockey.

'Always wanted to be a jockey. Right back as far as I can remember. Used to ride around on the dog at home. Straight. I gave him murder. He must have hated me. I think he had a nervous breakdown. Started thinking he was an horse. Like it here. Straight. Fresh air. They look after you all right an' all. Like the horses. Better than people. True. If I had to choose between horses and people I'd have the horses every time, no bother. You never know of a mare leaving a foal less she was made to. Never. Look at me. But I'm all right here. Like family, know what I mean?'

I offered him some of the pie he'd brought.

'No, you have it. I'm not supposed to eat. Got to keep my weight down. After a bit you don't notice being hungry. One day though, I'll win it. I'll win the National.' He shook his head and laughed. 'Just a dream,' he said. 'Anything you dream about?'

I thought for a second.

'Just to get my Dad back.'

'Yeah. Well, you cross your fingers for me and I'll do the same for you.'

He got up.

'Look, I got to go or they'll be wondering where I am. You'll be all right here tonight. Warm and dry. You won't mind the mice.'

'I haven't seen any mice yet.'

'Kept away from you so far. Pong kept 'em off. Now you smell good they'll be back. Company, see.' He laughed. Then immediately was serious. 'Now listen, tomorrow, right, I'm going to be up before everybody. It don't worry me, I'm used, see. I'm going to open the door and leave you to it. I can't been seen with you or I'm for it. All right. Now what you do is, I'll leave my bike in the lane. I'll leave it just behind the hedge as you go into the lane. There's a gate there. Now what you do is, you go down the lane and you come to a road. There'll be nobody about. If there is, just say Tony lent you his bike. Now you turn right and you'll come to the village. It's about a mile, mile and a half. There's only three shops. The bus stop is right outside the Post Office. That bus takes you to Southport. It's a 53B.'

'What about your bike?'

'I'll leave the padlock on the bike. The combination number is 5274. Right next to the Post Office is the Church, right. There's a little lane. Just lean it against the hedge. And don't forget to put the padlock on it. I don't want the bleeding Vicar pinching my bike.'

He looked at me. 'You got money?'

'I left it in the old trousers.'

'Lucky I asked.'

I took out the notes and offered him one.

'I didn't mean that. I was asking if you had enough. What you trying to do, insult me? Right, I'm off now. You going to be all right?'

'I'll be fine.'

'Yeah, well goodnight then. Don't forget the number on the padlock. 5274.' He banged me on the shoulder and went to the door. I could see his old, young head against the sky. He turned round.

'Here, what's your name?' he asked.

'Louie,' I said. 'Some people call me Lou.'

'That's why you smell so bad.'

'I'll send the coat and the trousers back in the post.'

'Forget it, pal. Exchange is no robbery. Especially when they weren't mine in the first place.'

'Tony,' I said. He looked back. 'I'll look out for you in the Grand National. When you win it.'

'I should be so lucky. See you pal.' And he was gone.

I wrapped the jacket round me and lay down in the straw. It smelled good and sweet. I could hear the hollow sound of the horse shifting. I played over the events of the day. I wondered where I'd be tomorrow. The hay seemed to be moving. The moon swung down slowly. There was my Dad pulling it down on a long string. He waved me over. I fell asleep

Chapter 9

The letters 'F' and 'L' were hanging loose so what it said was 'Oral Hall' not Floral Hall. I walked round trying all the doors but everywhere was locked up. I shaded my hand against windows. There was a corridor with carpet and some green plants. But I couldn't see anyone moving about. At the main entrance was a big poster with a picture of Murray Palermo smiling and playing his guitar. It was the same photograph that had been in the paper. Underneath it had written in big red letters:

AFTERNOON AND EVENING: 3.00 P.M AND 8.00 P.M.

The theatre was set among sunken gardens, full of flowers. In one of the beds was a huge clock all made of different flowers. It said half past eight. I walked up the promenade and sat down on a bench to wait. Somebody would be along soon. I got out the meat pie that Tony had given me. Everything had happened as he'd said it would. The bike had been there, the Post Office had been there and the bus had come. Soon I'd be seeing my Dad.

I said to myself, 'He's probably not here. It's only a guess that he's with Palermo. He's probably miles away. Maybe in another country.' I'd learned from what had happened in Birmingham. I was preparing myself for disappointment. A seagull fluttered down and sat on the back of the bench. I threw him a piece of meat pie. He picked it off the bench and flew off with it. Three more seagulls arrived. I finished the pie myself. I was hungry, too. I looked out to sea. Only there wasn't any sea. Just miles and miles of beach. Be no good if you went swimming. By the time you reached the water you'd be worn out. Over to the right, miles in the distance, was the faint outline of a tall tower. I wondered where it could be. Maybe it was the Eiffel Tower. Maybe that was France. Suddenly I feld cold. Two ladies in flowered hats and overcoats sat down on the bench and started speaking Welsh. Now and then there were bits of English. One with a handbag took out a photograph and showed it to the other. 'He's in Bangor Normal now. Studying Science.'

'Dear me Megan. He's getting on then.'

The other put the photo back in her handbag.

'Yes. They're all growing up.'

I wondered if Mum was talking about me to someone. I thought I'd phone her up before she went to work. I sneezed and pulled my coat round me and walked down the promenade looking for a phone box. I'd worked out what I would say each time. As soon as she answered I'd say, 'It's Louie, Mum. I'm all right. You're not to worry,' and then put the phone down. If she started talking and saying things, it just upset me.

After the pips stopped there was a long pause before she said, 'Hello'. It was as if she was expecting bad news. I spoke my line. As I put the phone down I heard her say, 'Oh Louie, it's just like your Dad all over again.' I said, 'Goodbye' and put the phone down. I wasn't really like my Dad, I thought. I just couldn't wait to get home. I didn't really like to be noticed. I didn't like being different. I couldn't stand it that most people had their dads there all the time and mine was always running away. I didn't want Uncle Edgar as a dad, but at least he was home all the time. When I was about nine and we'd gone on the camping trip with the cubs and everybody was waving to their dad, I felt everybody knew my dad wasn't there. So I'd waved and shouted. 'Goodbye Dad,' as the coach pulled out, even though I knew there was nobody there. Billy Fa Fa had turned round to me and said really loud so everybody could hear, 'What you shouting to your dad for? He's not there. You're mad Langton.' They'd all laughed. It still made me mad to think of that. I was glad I'd knocked half his tooth out. I should have knocked it all out.

'What?' said a man with an umbrella who was pushing past me into the telephone booth. I must have spoken out loud. Perhaps I was going funny.

'Nothing,' I said.

The sun was shining but I was feeling shivery. The back of my throat was burning and dry at the same time, the way it is just before you get a cold. I walked back towards the Floral Hall. The doors were open. A group of men in jeans and funny hats were carrying microphones and loud speakers through the doors. There was a big single decker bus down the side of the hall. On the side in big red letters was written MURRAY PALERMO. U.K. TOUR. Next to it was an American flag with a big microphone in front of it.

I walked up to the double doors. There was nobody about. I slipped inside. There was a thick brown capet on the floor. A man with keys jangling on his hip wearing a uniform and a cap came towards me down the corridor. With him was a smaller man in shirt sleeves. I slipped behind a curtain.

'Why is there nobody on these doors?' the man in shirt sleeves was saying.

'What are we supposed to do?' the man in the uniform said. 'There's only two of us.'

'Just have the one door open and everybody has to have a pass,' I heard the other one say as they disappeared round the corner. I stole out. The coast was clear. I felt my heart beating. Maybe somewhere in this building, my Dad was sitting. There was a distant booming like thunder. Outside the sun was shining really brightly.

I tiptoed down another corridor and opened a door. The thunder was louder. I was in the back of a theatre. I'd never been in one before when it was empty. Rows of seats stretched down towards a stage. Three men were pinning a huge banner across the back of it. In gold letters five feet tall was written MURRAY PALERMO and underneath in smaller letters: THE VIRGINIAN IS BACK IN TOWN.

Underneath the sign a dark, short man wearing a stetson and glasses was playing drums. That was the thunder I'd heard. Three or four other men were paying out cable and climbing on to speakers. One of them kept saying, 'One, two. One, two,' over and over again into a microphone.

I walked down an aisle ready to run if that security guard returned. Halfway down amongst all the seats was a huge table full of switches and dials. A man with long hair tied into a plait and wearing sunglasses kept moving sliders up and down and adjusting the knobs. He wore a T-shirt. On the back was written in red letters *The South's Gonna Rise Again*.

He called out to the drummer, 'OK. Mel, let me hear the toms.' He made a flurry with his hands as if he was playing a long row of drums. Mel began hitting the drums. It was so loud I put my fingers in my ears. The man at the desk didn't seem to notice how loud the noise was. Perhaps he knew where Dad was. I went up to him.

'Excuse me,' I shouted, 'I'm looking for my dad.'

He went on fiddling with the sliders as if he hadn't heard me.

I shouted louder, 'EXCUSE ME, I'M LOOKING FOR MY DAD.'

Just as I said it the drums went quiet. My voice rang round the hall.

'What?' said the man on the desk.

'Didn't say nothing,' said the drummer.

'Thought you said something.'

'Not a word, boy, not a word. It was the kid in back of you.'

The man at the desk turned towards me. 'What you want?' He didn't sound very pleased to see me.

'I'm looking for my dad,' I said.

'You what?'

He *was* deaf.

'MY DAD. I'M LOOKING FOR HIM.'

'Who?'

'MY DAD. I'M LOOKING FOR HIM.'

The man was fiddling with his desk again.

'Never heard of him,' he said without looking at me.

'He's called Harry Langton. He's. . .' I could see he couldn't hear. 'HE'S CALLED HARRY LANGTON, HE PLAYS IN THE BAND.'

'It's over there.'

'NO, MY DAD HE PLAYS IN THE BAND.'

'Let's hear the snare, Mel,' he shouted at the drummer. A tall bass player strolled on to the stage and began plucking at his guitar. The man at the desk turned to me. 'Bugger off, I'm busy.'

The drums exploded off the walls. I could feel the bass throbbing in my chest and through the balls of my feet.

108

'How's that?' shouted the drummer.

'Perfect,' said the soundman. He seemed to be able to hear clearly when the drums were playing.

I looked round the hall. Dad must be somewhere. A man with a transparent blue fiddle walked through some swing doors next to the stage. Dad must be through there somewhere. In the dressing rooms. 'Boom-be-Boom-Boom,' sang the bass guitar. The fiddle player had climbed on to the stage. There was no one about. I slipped through the swing doors and found myself in a long curved corridor. I walked down it a few steps. It was lined with mirrors. Then a door. Over it was written 'Artists Only'. That would be it. I pushed it open slowly and found myself in another empty corridor. On either side were doors. I walked down trying the doors. The first three were locked. The fourth one opened. Very slowly I pushed it. It was empty. Just a chair and a table with a mirror above it. Over the chair was a blue jacket. I backed out and closed the door.

'Here! What you doing?'

It was the security guard. I stood with my back to the door. He came over to me and looked down. He had onions on his breath and a short moustache. He sucked something through his teeth. It made a whistling noise.

'What you doing in that dressing room?'

'I was looking for my dad.'

He sucked his tooth again.

'Oh yeah. What you got in the bag?'

He took it off me and hauled out the contents. 'Looking for your dad?' Out came half a meat pie. A pair of underpants, two pairs of socks. 'Who's your dad then?'

'He plays in the band.'

'Oh yeah. Plays in the band, does he? What's his name?'

109

'Harry Langton.'

'Oh yeah.' He put the things back in my bag. 'Harry Langton. That your Dad, is it? Where's your Mum?'

'Home.'

'Where's that?'

'She sent me with a message. From the hotel.'

'Sent you with a message, did she?' He handed me back the bag.

'Yes.' I remembered the name of a hotel I'd seen on the Promenade. 'The Regent Hotel.'

'The Regent Hotel. I see.' He picked a piece of bacon out of his back tooth. Looked at it then flicked it away. 'Tell you what. Let's do this shall we, son. Let's go to my room. I got a nice little room. You'll like it there. It's got a phone. We can phone up your Mum. You'll enjoy doing that won't you?' He suddenly grabbed my arm and lifted me so that my toes were hardly touching the ground. I was looking straight into his face. And if she's not there sonny, if she's not there, that means you've been telling me lies and you'll be in trouble. Very serious trouble.' He let me go and started to walk up the corridor with me beside him. All the time he was asking questions. We passed another corridor branching off. I dropped a bit behind him. Not enough to make him suspicious but enough to slip off without him noticing. When we got to the corridor I stopped and slid down it. I could still hear him talking. I sprinted down the corridor. I heard him give a shout, and then he was after me. On my right was a door. I tried it. It was open and the room empty. I leant against the door holding my breath. I heard the guard charging past. He stopped. He was talking to somebody in the corridor. There was a table by a window. The curtains were drawn. On the dressing table were two glasses and a bottle of whisky. A cigar was burning in an ashtray. Whoever had been there was coming back soon. An open door on my right led into a smaller room. I heard the guard saying to someone in the corridor. 'See a boy come down here?'

A deep American voice said, 'Ain't seen nothing.'

'Mind if I take a look in your room?'

'Help yourself.'

The door handle turned. I raced on tiptoe through the other door. There was a bed with a white guitar and a stetson on it. In the corner was a hanging plastic curtain. I plunged behind the curtain. The floor was tiled. Water dripped from a spout above my head on to my boots. I was in a shower. There was a tiny hole in the curtain. Through it I could see the guard. With him was a large man with a large chest and broad shoulders. He was wearing high heeled boots and there was a large M.P. monogrammed on his white shirt. I'd seen that face before somewhere. Of course, the poster. It was him I was in Murray Palermo's shower. Murray poked his head round the smaller room. He was chewing on the big cigar. It smelled like Christmas.

'Ain't nobody hereabouts,' he said.

'Sorry to bother you Mr Palermo.'

'Be my guest.' The door closed. My feet were getting wet.

He whistled a tune then picked up a telephone. I tried to stop the drip by turning the handle but it made no difference.

'Hi! This is Murray . . . How y'all doin'. Now lookey here, I got a free day next week. I want to get in the studio. Get those tracks down.'

He had a funny accent. Every word seemed to have a 'y' in the middle of it. As he was talking he was sitting down

111

and taking off his boots. He took of his trousers and threw them into a corner.

'I have this song I want to do. One of the boys here wrote it. But I don't want to give him the idea that I like it over much, else he's gonna want payin' for it. And I sure have a prejudice 'bout payin' out for things. You understand what I'm telling you?'

He took off his shirt. There was a large corset round his waist. He undid the corset and the large chest became a low stomach. He walked round the room carrying the phone on a long lead, wearing his shorts, a cowboy hat and smoking a cigar. He came into the room where I was hiding. I cowered into the corner.

'So you tell him, if he says anything, that maybe we'll do it maybe we won't. He's desperate set on gettin' this song done. So we don't give him any points. Just put a couple of hundred bucks in his boot. He'll be happy. But you draw it up. You're the lawyer. That's what I pay you for. After that, it's my song. Ain't nobody's name going on that record but mine. That's how I've always done it and this old hoss is too old to change now, you hear me?'

A large hairy fist reached in past the curtain and turned on the water. It was like a rain storm. His hand reached for the curtain. There was a knock on the door.

'Yup,' said Murray.

The door opened.

'Can I have a word, Murray?'

'Sure.'

I hoped this wasn't going to be a long conversation. I wondered if you could drown standing up. I could see the water flooding out of my boots. Somewhere at the back of my nose a sneeze was gathering itself.

Murray had a towel round his waist. He was in the

112

interconnecting doorway. I couldn't see the other person. I heard his voice say, 'It's about the song. I wondered if you'd listened to the tape.'

'The song. Oh sure. It's O.K.'

'O.K.?'

'Yeah. Not too bad, not too good. Know what I'm saying?'

'D'you think you may put it on the album?'

'Hell, I don't know about that now. Ain't up to me. We have to talk royalties and stuff. Talk to the lawyer.'

'I see.'

There was something about the voice. I couldn't hear very well for the shower and the water running out of my ears.

'I'm going in the studio Monday. You know me, I make up my mind then. Why don't you come to the studio? We could sign it all up. Then I have to catch my flight.'

'Sure Murray. Thanks Murray.'

'My pleasure.'

I recognized that voice. It was Dad!

The sneeze was almost upon me. I squeezed my nose till it hurt. Murray pulled open the curtain. This time he was only wearing his stetson. The sneeze exploded all over him.

'What the Hell . . .'

I tried to squeeze past him but a big hand grabbed me.

'Dad!' I shouted.

'Didn't anybody tell you you're supposed to take your clothes off before you take a shower?'

'That's my dad,' I called.

Suddenly, there he was standing in the doorway. He was wearing a blue suit with silver buttons. It was strange to see him like that: like other people saw him. He was even more surprised to see me standing there, fully clothed in a shower.

'Louie!' he said. He walked towards me as if he'd seen a ghost. 'How . . . what . . . Louie.' He didn't know which question to ask first. Murray Palermo almost lifted me out on to the carpet.

'You're soaking wet,' said Dad. There was a river running out of my boots. He got hold of my shoulders and looked at me. He still couldn't believe it.

'Ain't surprised,' said Murray. 'Boy's been standing in my shower with his clothes on. Must be the guy security was looking for. You know him?'

'It's my son,' said Dad and drew me to him. I liked it when he said that.

'This is your boy?'

'How did you get here for goodness sake?' asked Dad.

'I was looking for you, Dad.'

Murray looked at me and shook his head. 'You were lookin' for your daddy in my shower?' I was shaking. My teeth were rattling.

'Dad,' I said. 'You've got to come home.' I started telling him about Uncle Edgar and Jo and the fire and everything but I couldn't get the words out for shivering.

Dad put his arms around me.

Murray said, 'Why don't you get the boy back to your room?' He looked at the puddle on his carpet. 'He ain't well and if he hangs around here much longer we're all gonna have to swim for it.'

Dad lifted me up. 'Can I take the bus back to the hotel, Murray? I don't want him catching pneumonia.'

'Sure, but pick up the boys for the afternoon show.'

Dad rushed me out into the corridor and into the bus.

A quarter of an hour later I was sitting up in bed in Dad's hotel room drinking hot milk and eating a sandwich.

Chapter 10

'Here, take these,' said Dad. He held out two pills in the palm of his hand.

I swallowed them down one after the other and washed them down with the warm milk.

'Maybe make you sweat. Get your temperature down.' He put his palm against my forehead. I remembered him doing that when I was supposed to be going to school and I would hope I was ill enough to have to stay at home. I was wearing a long red shirt of Dad's. It came down to my knees. We looked at each other and both nodded and smiled. I took another gulp of milk. There was something strange about being there in the room with him. He was the reason I'd travelled all that distance; had all those adventures. It had all been for him. But now I'd found him at last, I wasn't sure what to say. I didn't know where to start. It was so comfortable sitting up in that bed in a warm hotel room that I didn't want to start talking about things that might upset him. It was like being in a sort of nowhere. Dad was watching me. I had a feeling he knew what I was thinking.

'This your room?' I asked.

He gave a little nod of his head. 'Yes, this is it.'

I looked round over the edge of the mug. It was like somebody's bedroom except there was a small bathroom through a door at one side. There were clothes on the floor and an open suitcase by the wardrobe. On the dressing table was a pile of cassettes and some cups and dirty plates on a tray. Over the radiator near the bathroom my clothes were steaming. I looked back at Dad.

'You've grown a moustache,' I said.

He stroked it and smiled. It was droopy and black. There were flecks of grey in it. 'Cowboy style,' he said.

I took another drink. 'Was that Murray?' I asked.

'That was him. Murray Palermo.'

I thought of him striding round talking into the telephone and taking his shirt off.

'He wears a corset,' I said. 'I saw him take it off.'

'You always had all the luck,' said Dad.

'He's got a great big belly.'

'Big bank roll too.'

It was good talking with Dad. There were lots of pauses but it wasn't embarrassing like it would be with Uncle Edgar. Dad had a way of being very still when he wanted to. It kept you calm. He had these wrinkles round his eyes that made him look as if he was smiling even when he wasn't.

'Are you immature for your age?'

He raised his eyebrows. 'Who's been flattering me?'

'Uncle Edgar. He said some men when they saw they were getting near forty, they wanted to go back to how they were, when they were younger.'

He didn't get upset. I could see him rolling it about in his mind quite seriously. 'Immature?' he repeated. 'I suppose I am. Thank God!'

'I wouldn't want to be mature if it meant being like Uncle Edgar.' I wondered what the opposite of immature was. What was the word for behaving old even when you were young?

'Uncle Edgar's a clever man. He's probably right.'

'I saw the band practising. Are they good?'

116

'Sound check,' said Dad. 'They do that to make sure all the instruments are balanced. It's a good band.'

He took the mug off me and put it on the bedside table.

'D'you like it with the band? You know, travelling round.'

'It gets into your blood. It can be hard to get used to anything else.'

'Do they think you're a good player? A good guitarist?'

Dad had pulled his shirt off. He was washing his face in the sink. He cupped water on both hands and splashed it over his face and the back of his neck. He dried himself with a towel. He laughed and shook his head.

'I'm what they call,' he thought about it for a minute watching his face in the mirror, 'I'm what they call the driving force of the band. The driving force behind the whole unit. I'm the one who keeps it moving.'

'I saw your fingernail.'

He pulled a clean shirt over his head. 'What?'

'In the photo. You'd grown your fingernail so you could play better.'

'Ah.' He closed his right hand into a fist. I noticed the nail that had once been long was as short as the others.

I said, 'I suppose when you get back into practice, playing with a band all the time, it doesn't matter so much.'

'Something like that,' he said.

He was looking out of the window doing up his cuffs and then buttoning up the suit with silver buttons.

'That's how I guessed where you'd be. I saw the cassette in the shed. It had your song on it. I found out you were in Southport from the paper. At first I thought Palermo was a place in Italy.'

'Sherlock Holmes eh?'

117

'I went to Birmingham but you weren't there.'

'I'm amazed that you've found me.'

He sat on the edge of my bed.

'If I ask you something, you won't laugh, will you?'

'Certainly not.'

I'd remembered when we'd been going to the hospital. 'What were you thinking about on the 5th July at about half past five in the afternoon?'

'What was I thinking about? Mmh. We were in Germany, weren't we?

'We go to all these N.A.T.O. bases. Lot of Americans out there. Starved of Country Music. Maybe it was Italy. I've travelled all over. What were you thinking about?'

'I was in a car and I was thinking that I'd like you to be thinking about me. I thought if I thought hard enough I could make anybody think what I was thinking.'

'Mmh. Well I probably was thinking about you. You or Jo or Mum.'

I thought about that.

'Is that good enough?'

I thought it probably was. He brushed the hair out of my eyes.

'Does Mum know you're here?'

'I ring her every day.'

He picked up the phone. 'Maybe you ought to phone her now.'

'I rang her this morning. I didn't tell her where I was. Just told her . . .'

'You were still alive.'

'Yes.'

He put the phone down gently.

'We'll ring her later,' he said.

He got up. 'You lie there and sweat if you can. I don't

want to go. But I have my job to do. You understand don't you?'

'Driving force behind the band.'

'You just lie there.'

He switched on the television.

'Can I come?' I asked.

He shook his head.

'Tonight?'

'Maybe. We'll see how you are.'

He tucked me down into the bed.

'You watch the television. It's Saturday. Maybe there'll be wrestling on.'

He ran his fingers through my hair.

'I won't be long.'

There was an old black and white movie on. One set of cowboys was chasing another across a desert. You could see the white smoke puffing out of their revolvers. The sound was turned down. Now and then a horse died and a rider rolled into the dust.

Dad was at the door. 'If you want anything, just ring that bell. I've told them at the desk. They know you're here. If you're really bad, I've told them to get me at the theatre. But I think you'll be OK.'

He gave the sign he always did when he was leaving. It had started as a joke but now we always did it. He held up his palm and turned it in a circle.

There was something I wanted to know.

'Dad,' I said. 'Are you coming back? Are you going to come home?'

He turned and looked at me. 'We can't talk about it now. We need time to talk about it properly. We said that, didn't we. I want to hear everything you've done.

119

Everything that's been happening at home.' He paused. 'It's hard for me too. We'll talk about it later.'

'Yeah, later,' I said.

He went out, closing the door quietly.

Suddenly it was quiet. It reminded me of those times when I'd been out in that bus with Dad. Sometimes after driving a few hundred miles when he'd dropped everyone off and we were on our way back to the garage or to our old house, he'd stop the bus and climb down to get some sweets or a present for Mum. I'd be left on my own in the bus. After the noise of the tyres and the engine rumbling and shaking and Dad talking, everything would go really quiet. It was funny really. Well, that's how I felt in that hotel room after Dad had left to go to the show.

I watched the TV in a blank kind of way, not really taking in what was going on. The gang had reached the hills. There was a big river. Someone looked over a huge ravine. A cowboy came into close up. He wasn't wearing a gun but he faced the big gang. I had a feeling I'd seen the film before. Then, I saw one of the gang crawling across the edge of the cliff. I jumped out of bed and turned up the sound. I jerked open the door and ran to the stairs.

'Dad, Dad,' I shouted. 'It's the film where he goes over. It's the film where you speak.'

But he'd gone. I ran back to the room and over to the window. Down below in the street the big bus was pulling out into the traffic. I sat on the edge of the bed. Everything was exactly how he'd explained it. Then came the line.

'Biggest drop I ever saw.'

It was a great line. I couldn't stop myself laughing. My eye caught a large yellow card on the top of the set. It said:

MURRAY PALERMO IN CONCERT
FLORAL HALL SOUTHPORT
SATURDAY JULY 30TH. COMPLIMENTARY ADMIT ONE.

It couldn't be far to the Floral Hall. I went over to where my clothes were. They were still damp. I looked at my face in the mirror. I wondered if I looked different, after all the things that had happened. But I didn't. Just a bit whiter. I didn't feel so bad. There was a pair of Dad's jeans in the drawer. I pulled them up over the long red shirt. They were too big round the waist and came over the ends of my boots, but when I'd put a belt round and rolled the bottoms up they were all right. I had dry socks in my bag. Money? What if they wouldn't let me in? Even with that special ticket? I felt in the pocket of my trousers and pulled out the money. It was wringing wet. But there wasn't a law against damp money. I slipped the notes into my pocket, picked up the spare room key that Dad had left me and slipped out into the street.

At the Floral Hall there wasn't any trouble with the ticket. The man on the door just tore it in half and I was shown to an aisle seat about half way down. Music was playing but the curtains were drawn and the lights were up all over the audience. Most of them seemed to be older than me. Some of them wore cowboy shirts. One or two of the men wore big hats. I sat next to a man with glasses; there was a younger woman of about twenty five on the other side of him. I think she must have been his daughter. She was eating chocolates. I wanted to tell somebody that I'd run away from home to find my Dad. But I knew that would be stupid. I leant across to the man.

'My Dad's in the band,' I said. 'He writes some of the songs.'

121

'What did he say?' said the girl. Her mouth was full of chocolate.

The man said, 'He says his dad's in the band.'

'Oooh,' said the girl and looked at me. She popped another chocolate in her mouth.

'Do you know him?'

'Of course.'

'No, Murray. D'you know Murray Palermo?'

'I was in his shower this morning.'

'Ooh,' said the girl. 'I love him. Think he's great.'

A loud voice came from somewhere.

'And now, Ladies and Gentlemen, we are proud to present Live in Concert for the First Time in Britain, Ladies and Gentlemen put your hands together for the Virginian himself, In Person, the one and only Murray Palermo.'

The audience whistled and clapped and the curtains shot up as the drums crashed and all the band played. It was different from seeing it in the morning. There were bright, coloured lights beamed all over the stage and the big sign at the back had turned a deep red colour. Murray Palermo strode on from the side of the stage, waving at the audience. He was wearing the big hat I'd seen in his changing room and had the guitar round his neck on a gold strap. Round his waist was a huge belt.

He laughed at the audience and said, 'How you all doin'?' and then went into the first song. It was Dad's song. The one I'd heard Jo playing on the cassette that day. It sounded completely different in the Hall. The whole concert was different. Like seeing a film in colour instead of black and white.

When he finished the song Murray hitched up his trousers and said, 'Thank you, thank you kindly. Why we love you.'

122

The audience roared. I wondered if I was the only one who knew he was wearing a corset.

I leaned across to the girl in glasses, 'That song he just sang, my Dad wrote it.'

I could hear her saying 'Ooh' in the darkness. 'Think he's really great.'

All this time I was peering as hard as I could at the stage trying to pick out Dad. Most of the light was on Murray. Everything was in darkness except for the spotlight on him.

He said, 'Heah's a song that did real good for me about five year ago.' The guitar played the introduction and the bass boomed in over the drums. 'Guess I have to thank each and every one of you for making it a hit. It's called, You sent your Heart in a Letter.'

He closed his eyes and the big voice came out. It sounded as if he was almost going to cry at one point. The guitar player took a solo and the lights came up brighter. That wasn't Dad. I looked at each of the musicians in turn. I couldn't understand it. I counted them all again, in case I'd missed someone out. He still wasn't there. What had happened to him?

The girl leaned across, 'Which one is he?' she asked.

He wasn't there.

I pointed to a big man in a big straw stetson playing the fiddle.

'The one playing the fiddle,' I said. I crept out of the theatre and into the street. The sun made me blink after the darkness of the theatre. I could hear the audience cheering and whistling as I walked towards the rails by the sand. The cheering grew fainter. Then the music started. I looked round. I could see the tour bus. It was pulled up in a lay-by against the stage door. The driver was sitting in it, reading a paper. All sorts of thoughts were buzzing through my mind. I couldn't understand why Dad hadn't been there. What had happened to him? I'd seen him drive off in the bus. Maybe he was ill? Perhaps seeing me had frightened him and he'd run off again. Perhaps he hated being at home with us so much, he'd run off and gone into hiding again. What was the point of me chasing after him if he really didn't want to come home? I remembered something my mother had said once to Auntie Edith. She'd been mad because he hadn't been there when Jo was born. She'd said, 'I'd rather have him somewhere else and happy than here and miserable and blaming me for it.' I understood now what she meant. Maybe he was a wanderer? He'd told me once he'd been running away from home since he was two. If he passed a train with the door open or a bus standing at a stop he couldn't resist jumping on board. If you asked him why, he'd just smile and say, 'To see where it was going.'

Perhaps it would be better to ring up Mum and catch the next train home. What was the point of dragging Dad home against his will? Like Mum said, 'A rolling stone never changes its spots.'

The bus driver turned over a page. Maybe he knew where Dad was. I walked round to the front of the bus. A police car swept up the promenade with its lights flashing. I wondered if they were looking for me. I shouted through the windscreen, but the driver didn't hear me. I shouted louder and hammered on the bonnet. He lowered the paper and I saw Dad's face looking down at me. For what seemed a long time we just stared at one another. It was as if my mind had gone blank. Then all sorts of thoughts started chasing each other round my brain. It was like a pin-ball machine where the ball keeps setting off one light after another. Flash. But that answer only leads to another question. Flash. He's missed the concert. Flash. Why's he sitting in the bus? Flash. That's why he had the bus before; he was the driver. The driving force behind the band. Flash. I'd asked him and he'd avoided the question. It was a lie. My Dad had told me a lie. Just to make himself look good. I didn't mind him being the bus driver. What was wrong with being a bus driver? I'd liked it when we'd gone round together. Better than being a liar.

Somebody was shouting, 'Liar.' People were looking round to see who it was. It was me. I was banging on the bonnet with both fists shouting, 'Liar!' at the top of my voice. 'Liar!'

Dad was climbing out of the bus.

'Louie.'

Then I was running. Running I didn't know where. Pushing and scrambling past people and prams and faces. I just knew I had to keep running. It didn't matter where. Just run, that was all. I didn't know if he was chasing me. I didn't want him back. They'd been right. Uncle Edgar and all of them. Whatever they'd said. It had all been right. I collided with a pram coming the other way and spun across into a waste paper basket and on to the gravel. I could feel the blood on my leg and hand. But I didn't feel the pain.

And then I was on the beach and the sea was creeping up to my feet. I could hardly gulp the air into my lungs and the sea kept coming up to my feet. All the time moving. Moving backwards and forwards. It made a hissing sound. A soft, hissing whisper. It was as though it was saying something. Whispering one word over and over in my ear. And the word the sea was saying was, 'Lies, lies lies.'

Chapter 11

There was a man throwing sticks for a long haired mongrel. Over and over again he threw them, and every time the dog plunged out into the sea and then scampered across the sand before laying the stick at his master's feet. Then off he'd go again. With his fur wet, there wasn't much of him. He looked as if he was about to drop dead. But that didn't stop him running and swimming. What a stupid way to carry on, I thought. I'd rather be dead than spend my life doing that. And then I thought, my life wasn't all that different; everybody was chasing some kind of stick. Pity though that you couldn't change parts. I was stuck with being me all my life. What if the dog was to start throwing the sticks and his master had to chase after them? I wondered if it was possible to change. To become someone else. Maybe I had. Maybe I had changed over the last few days. The thing was the change was so slow you didn't notice it.

A plane droned overhead. It was one of those old fashioned planes that took sightseers round the bay and over the town for fifteen minutes. It had a banner trailing out behind. it. The banner said in big letters, 'Come To Sunny Southport'. It seemed to be travelling very slowly.

There was a scratching noise behind me. I looked round. It was Dad. He had a piece of wood in his hand. He was writing something very carefully in the sand. He had his back to me. He'd written a big letter 'L'. It was about three yards long. Then he wrote an 'O'. He was writing my name. I turned out to sea, before he noticed I'd seen what he was doing . . .

The man and his dog had wandered off . . .

The scratching in the sand stopped. I could feel Dad was quite close to me. I just kept looking out at the clouds piled up beyond the grey, flat water.

'Remember that summer we went to Jersey and all wrote our names in the sand. You and me and Mum and Jo. Nearly covered the whole beach.'

I just kept looking straight out. The scratching started again. I wondered which letter he'd got up to.

'Covered half the beach by the time we'd finished. It was you who made us do it. You said it had to be big enough to be read by an aeroplane in case we needed to be rescued. I remember you wanted to put S.O.S. but your Mum wouldn't let you in case anybody thought we really were in trouble. Just like your mother that.'

The plane went past again.

'Think you'd be able to read this from up there?'

I just kept looking straight ahead. I didn't want to talk to him.

'Louie? D'you think you'd be able to read your name from up there?'

'I don't know.' I hadn't meant to sound sulky but that's how it came out. He was standing close behind me now. I just wanted to be on my own. I had a lot to think about, to work out.

'Something the matter?'

'No.'

'Tell me about it.'

'No.'

'It's no good standing here.'

'You know.'

127

'I don't know. Tell me.'

The plane was taking off again. It taxied along the beach. Then slowly lifted off. It seemed to take a long time before it was really in the air.

'You lied to me,' I said.

'How did I lie?'

'You know.'

'I don't know. You'll have to tell me.'

'Yes you did, you know you did. You lied about the band. About playing in the band.'

'Did I?'

'Course you did. I went in this afternoon. I went to see the show. I told this lady you were in the band. You weren't there.'

'Ah.'

'You told me you were in the band.'

'I never said I was in the band.'

'You did.'

'I said I was the driving force behind the band. Well, I am. I drive the band everywhere.'

'You know what you meant me to think.'

There was a pause. Then Dad said quietly, 'Are you ashamed of me being a bus driver?'

'You should have told me. It wouldn't bother me your being a bus driver. What you shouldn't have done was to lie.'

'The trouble is that people expect too much of each other. Especially their dads. What you wanted was for me to be a star musician. It's no good shaking your head. You did. That's why you asked those questions . . . Do they think you're a good guitar player? You expect too much of me. Then when I don't come out as great as you want me to be, you feel let down.'

It was true, I had wanted him to be good. 'But you started all that. Writing all those letters. Taking me to see all those films you were in,' I said.

'That's true. But Louie, every dad wants to be a hero for his son.'

'I didn't want you to be a hero. I wanted you to be there. Like everybody else's dad. That's all Mum wanted too.'

'I see.'

'You should have told me. It doesn't matter to me what you do. I'd like it if you were a good actor or a musician. Yes, I'd like that but it doesn't really matter. Not really. I didn't want, what I didn't want was for you to lie.'

We were standing shoulder to shoulder. Both looking straight out. Not looking at one another at all but we were both talking really hard. The tide was creeping in. But neither of us wanted to move back. I felt if I worried about my boots getting wet it would make what I was saying less important.

Dad sighed and scratched his head. 'You know,' he said slowly, 'just because I'm your father you shouldn't expect me to be perfect. I'm nothing special, I know that. Don't play guitar too well. I've got a pretty rotten voice, I suppose. I'm not even much of an actor, although I thought I was at one time, when I was eighteen. I suppose I haven't made much of a job of being a father. I'm just another bloke, that's all. I've spent my life trying to find something I was good at. To make up for everything else I made a mess of. But I never found it. And I'm not getting younger, so I suppose I never will now. But don't make your standards too high just because I'm your dad. I'm just like anybody else. Perhaps that's what it's taken me all these years to find out.'

129

'I don't care about everybody else. I don't want you like them. I want you to be better.'

Dad looked at me. 'How can I be better?'

'By telling the truth,' I shouted.

Suddenly I was hitting him with both hands. He held me at a distance but I kept on striking him on the chest and shoulders. Everything I'd been keeping back came out. About Mum and how she'd been taken to hospital and Jo and the cupboard and how she'd stolen money and then set her bed on fire and how Uncle Edgar was round all the time and was trying to get Mum to divorce him and how I'd seen him that night asking Mum to marry him and she was seriously thinking about it. That it was all his fault, because he should have been there because if he had, none of it would have happened and when he'd gone before, at least he'd written but now he didn't even do that. I must have gone on for about ten minutes without drawing breath. When I'd finished I just stood there, shaking. Dad kept holding me. Just holding me very still. The plane flew in low over the sea. I could see the people's heads at the portholes. I wondered if they could see us, could see Dad holding me by the arms like that. It landed behind us, bouncing along the sand until it stopped.

When I'd stopped shaking, Dad said, 'Well it looks as if I've got a lot to answer for.' He gave me a big blue handkerchief. And I blew my nose. I'd stopped shaking. He told me to keep the handkerchief.

'Do I get a chance to defend myself?'

I nodded.

'I did write you know. I told her what was happening. Where I was. She wrote back and told me not to get in touch. She said it was upsetting for you and Jo when I kept coming and going. You see she thought I was back for good this last time. So did I. And I tried you know. I really did try.'

'I know,' I said.

'But it was Mum who didn't want me back this time. She needed time to think. I suppose she was right really. But something pulled me away. It was something I just had to do.'

He looked round. People were queuing to go into the plane.

'How can I explain it to you?' His eyes fixed on the plane. I saw that look come into them. When he has an idea, his eyes turn to windows. 'Ever been up in a plane?'

'No,' I said.

'Come on, race you to the plane.'

He was off and I couldn't catch him. He could really run too. We left two rows of footprints across my name in the sand.

We joined the queue. There was a post stuck in the sand. It said, 'See Southport and Blackpool from the air. Round trip, Five Pounds.'

Dad put his arm round my shoulders. There was a haze of heat coming off the plane and it smelled of oil and fuel. You could see where new bits had been riveted on to patch up the bodywork. The tyres were like doughnuts. It didn't look too safe to me. Two quite old ladies stood in front of me in the queue. They were laughing and talking about parachutes. I tried to look as if I went up in a ricketty old plane every day of my life. There were some wooden stairs you climbed up to a doorway. A man in white pumps and a peaked cap was collecting the money. He asked everybody how much they weighed before he let them in. When we got in, it smelled like an old bus. The carpets on the floor were all worn and split. The pilot was sitting at the

131

front. He turned round in his seat, watching us. I thought he would have goggles and headphones and be wearing a fleece-lined leather jacket. But he was dressed in ordinary clothes as if he was taking the family swimming or something. All the time he talked he looked really serious, so you couldn't tell if he was joking or not.

'All made your wills, have you?' he said.

The lady in front of me laughed but her friend said, 'Oh dear.'

'No, I'm only joking,' said the pilot. 'I can't help joking when I've been in the pub all day.'

Dad got me a seat against the bulkhead. The pilot started the engine. The whole plane shook. I could see the wings shivering and smoke coming from the propellors.

'Anybody here flown before?' asked the pilot.

Three people put their hands up. I was one of them.

'Don't worry, this could be your last.'

'All right?' asked my dad. He pulled the safety belt tight.

'I'm all right,' I said. I didn't feel it. I could see the headlines.

BOY AND FATHER KILLED IN TRAGIC RESORT AIR CRASH

The engines revved. Something fell off the luggage rack with a crash.

'Don't worry, it's only the engine,' said the pilot.

We rolled bumpily across the sand. The plane swayed from side to side. We began to accelerate. There was a lot of noise but the plane didn't seem to go much faster. The seats shook. Then we were off the ground but the plane didn't seem to rise very high. We travelled quite a distance and I could still see the sand about twenty feet beneath us.

My knuckles gripped the arms of my seat. I half sat up to help the plane get higher.

'If you could all throw your shoes overboard,' said the pilot.

Dad smiled at me. Then suddenly we were higher. The noise of the engine got less and the seats stopped rattling. We were banking over the sea. I wasn't scared any more. It just seemed exciting, like a dream. I thought to myself that we were probably going to crash but in a funny way it didn't bother me. Dad pointed out of the porthole. The horizon dipped and we glided in over the town. You could see the streets and the cars streaming by. Hundreds of people round a small patch of green that was a football ground.

'There's the Floral Hall.' I said to Dad. People were coming out and moving in different directions. The sea looked flat and wrinkled like a piece of grey paper.

'Blackpool Tower,' said my Dad.

'I thought it was the Eiffel Tower.' Dad laughed.

We weren't embarrassed with each other any more. I had a feeling it was going to be all right.

Dad leaned towards me. He had to shout above the hum of the engine.

'I wanted to try to explain to you. I suppose I haven't been much of a father, have I? So, well, I wanted to explain why I went off like that. It's not an excuse. Just to try to make you understand.'

He pointed down out of the porthole.

'All those houses.'

I knew what he meant.

'And in every one of them people.'

I'd often thought about that myself but I'd never told anybody because I thought they'd laugh. In every house

133

there would be people who had a life; just like I had. But I didn't know anything about them. And that was just one street. What about all those people in England and then in the world. It made you dizzy and sad to think about it. All the people that you'd never know anything about. And terrible things happening to them, all the time. All that, not knowing.

'Looks all right from up here, doesn't it? But if you were to go down into those houses they'd be just like everywhere else. People quarrelling or being happy now and then and going to work and coming home. D'you understand what I'm saying?'

I nodded.

'Then you think of all the stars. Millions and millions. More than you could count in a thousand lifetimes. And then think of all the people who've ever lived on earth. Millions of years. Just think of all those people.'

I was feeling dizzy again.

'Makes you feel very small. Me anyway.'

'Me too,' I said. Nobody had ever spoken to me like this before. It made me feel important that Dad was telling me all these things.

'Think of all the things going on. People washing their hair; arguing because someone hasn't put the top back on the toothpaste; things like that.'

I looked down and imagined all those things going on, underneath all those roofs.

'But up here, you're all right. It's the distance that does it. That's what I always felt. That's what made me leave. It doesn't mean that I don't love you and Jo and Mum, it's just that I was too close to it all. When I thought of things far away they looked clean and magical.' He laughed. 'But they're not. It's just the same once you get to look at it close up. It's taken me forty years to see that.'

The plane banked and flew low across the beach.

'Look,' I shouted, 'where you wrote my name.'

The sea was washing over the big letters Dad had drawn.

'That's what I could never stand. That you could live your life, do all the things that people do and then, it's all washed away.'

I could even see our footsteps leading away. They'd last a bit longer.

'That's why I tried to get into films I suppose. I thought it was fame and money but it wasn't really. Not underneath. That's why I came after Murray. Think of all those people, you know what I'm saying, those people we'll never know. And one day a few of them put on a record and they listen to my song. And they like it. It says something to them about their lives. And because they like it they go over to the record and look who wrote it, who wrote that song. And in little letters between two brackets read out my name. You understand? My name, Louie. Even if only a thousand did it. Five hundred. Even one! That would be really something, wouldn't it, Louie? Wouldn't it? That's all I wanted. That's all. Doesn't sound much to ask for, does it? But it would mean everything to me.'

Dad stopped. He looked at the lines on the palms of his hands. 'Is this making sense?'

'Yes,' I said, 'I know what you mean. Really.'

'Well, I was getting on to forty. Seems a long way away for you but the older you get the faster the years come tumbling. And I thought, you know, it's not going to happen. I tried to settle down. I really tried this last time. You don't know how I tried to become a steady nine-to-five man, with a steady nine-to-five mind. And I could have done it. It's not that I feel better than those people but there was always this thought at the back of my mind that another chance might come along. That it wasn't all over. Then out of the blue this album of Murray's came into my hands. It had that song on it. My song. I wrote it when we were both going around Tennessee together, singing songs wherever anyone would let us. We were terrible. Maybe if we'd carried on something would have happened. It did for him. I came home because I thought you needed me. You don't have to blame yourself. Anyway Murray stuck it out and now he's a star. Good luck to him. He deserves it. But he shouldn't have put my song on his album without my name. He shouldn't have done that. But there's nothing I can do about it now. But I've got another song. A good song too. And he knows it. In his heart Murray knows he stole that song. He knows he owes me. So on Monday he'll do my song. Put it on a record. Once that's out there'll be others. Once you get Murray Palermo to sing one of your songs a lot of people come knocking at your door. I won't need to go away again. I can sit in that little shed in the garden, write my songs and send them out. They'll do my wandering for me. But even if it's just that *one* song. That'll be enough for me. It's not money. It's not fame. It's leaving something. Something the sea can't wash away.'

He stopped talking and just looked straight ahead. The plane came in for its landing. I heard the wheels drop with a thump. We bounced on the sand and slowly came to a halt. The engine clattered into silence.

I looked at Dad. 'Does that mean you're coming home?' I asked.

He laughed a lot at that.

136

We walked across the sand towards the town.

'Yes, I'm coming home. If your mother will have me. I'd better ask her about that, hadn't I?'

Back at the hotel Dad made a cup of tea and walked about the room a lot. I could tell he was worried about making the telephone call to Mum. He'd forgotten I didn't drink tea so I knew he was nervous. Although it tasted horrible I drank it because I didn't want to disturb him. He took off his shoes and lay on the bed thinking. Then he picked up the phone. It was funny only hearing one side of the conversation. I had to guess what Mum was saying. I heard the sound of Mum saying 'Hello.' But mostly I could just hear the sound of her voice, not what she was saying.

'It's me . . . Harry . . . Yes. He's here now . . . Fine . . . In Southport . . . Honestly he's fine . . . in an aeroplane . . . an aeroplane . . . Who's that . . . Edgar? . . . What's he doing there? . . . I know . . . Louie told me . . . well you're not having a divorce . . . because I don't want to . . . because I love you . . . You can't marry him . . . because he can't make you laugh like I can . . . Or cry . . . It would be like marrying a packet of cornflakes . . . only a bit less exciting . . . Tell him to leave . . . yes now . . . I don't want him in my house . . . your house . . . Clear off Edgar . . . I'm coming home . . . Yes . . . Monday . . . Because I have to go into the studio . . . It's near London . . . He'll be with me . . . Can we talk about it Monday? It's important . . . It's only three more days . . . Once I've got this song down . . . I won't want to wander off again . . . No I won't . . . I've been thinking about it a lot . . . Can we talk on Monday . . . I know I've said it before but this time I mean it . . . I know I've said I mean it before but this time I really mean it. I really mean it . . . Yes . . . She wants to talk to you, Louie. Yes. Goodbye.'

He handed me the phone.

'Hello, Mum.'

'Are you all right?'

'Yes. We're going to the concert tonight.'

'How's your Dad? Is he eating properly?'

Dad looked at me and puffed out his cheeks and held his hands out round his stomach.

'He's getting quite fat.'

'Jo wants to ask you something.'

There was a lot of crackling as the phone was put down and picked up again. Then I heard Jo's voice.

'Hello.'

'Hello.'

'Hello.'

'Hello.'

'Have you got me the chocolates?'

'Yes.'

'Goodbye.'

I heard the phone put down.

That night I saw the whole of the concert. When Murray sang Dad's song I didn't clap. I just sat back and listened to the rest of the audience cheering. But Dad, he clapped along with everybody else. While he was clapping he didn't let on that he'd written the song. He just turned to the people on either side and said, 'Good song, isn't it. Yeah, good song.'

He hadn't really changed.

Chapter 12

In the studio it was 12.00 o'clock and Murray Palermo still hadn't arrived. They'd been waiting for him since 10.30. The band sat in the recording room, smoking, reading newspapers and talking. The engineer turned away from the sound desk on his swivel chair and looked at Dad.

'Isn't this your song?' he asked.

Dad nodded.

'Why don't you go in and sing it? Give the band a chance to get used to it. I can balance the sound.'

'If you think it would help,' said Dad.

'When Murray comes, he can walk straight into it.'

'O.K.' said Dad.

The engineer pressed a button and spoke into a small microphone.

'O.K. boys, we're going to take one. Give you all something to do.'

Dad walked into the studio. The musicians picked up their instruments; put down their newspapers. He stood by the microphone and held a set of headphones to his ears.

'Speak to me,' said the engineer.

Dad sang softly, 'I loved you the first time I saw you.'

'Just what I wanted to hear at 12.00 o'clock in the morning,' said the engineer.

The drummer played a staccato run across the skins of

139

his drum kit. The engineer pressed a button and the large reels of tape began to revolve.

'Let's go for it,' said the engineer, 'Crazy Like the Moon, take one.'

The piano player counted, 'One-Two-Three-Four.' On the fourth count all the band played the introduction. Dad's voice came through the loudspeakers. He didn't really have a good voice but he knew what the song was about. I sat on this low sofa and kept quiet like Dad had told me to.

A man in shirtsleeves and a waistcoat came through a door at the side, followed by two other men. One had a camera.

'Murray arrived yet?' he asked.

'No,' said the engineer. 'Should have been here at half past ten.'

'Search me,' said the engineer.

'When he comes in, tell him I've got these agreements for him to sign will you? These two guys are from the *Daily News*.' He went out.

'That's not Palermo singing, is it?' said the reporter.

The photographer sat next to me. 'Got a horrible voice whoever it is,' he said.

'It's my dad,' I said.

'Oh yeah,' said the reporter. 'He's still got a horrible voice.'

'He wrote the song,' I said. 'He's not supposed to be a singer.'

'You can say that again,' said the reporter.

'I quite like his voice,' said the engineer.

'No accounting for taste,' said the reporter. He took out a pen and notebook. 'Write a lot of songs does he, your Daddy?'

140

'He used to,' I said. 'He wrote stories too. Funny stories. Adventures. He's been a film actor too. He acted with John Wayne. With lots of big stars. Mr Palermo stole one of his songs. Dad doesn't mind him singing them but he wants his name there, on the record.'

'Might be a story there Eddie,' said the photographer. 'He wrote stories for his children, now pens the songs the stars sing. That kind of angle.'

Eddie put away his note book. 'No,' he said, 'the story's about Palermo. Not some nowhere song-writer.'

The song ended and Dad came through the door. 'How was it?' he asked.

'Diabolical,' said the photographer.

'What's so wonderful about perfection anyway?' said the engineer.

'How would you know?' said the journalist.

The engineer ran back the tape.

'Could you let me have a copy on tape?' Dad asked. 'You know, just for the record.'

'No problem,' said the engineer and wound some tape on to a machine.

Dad said to me, 'D'you want a drink?'

We walked through the studio and into the big reception area near the front door. The floor was made of tiles and there was a coloured fountain playing in the middle of the hall. Gold and yellow fish swam about in the pool. Out of the speakers came Dad's version of the song. Dad put some coins into the drink vending machine. Two paper cups dropped down. One filled with coffee and the other with coke.

Suddenly the main doors swung open and Murray Palermo strode through the hall and into the studio, followed by a small dark man in jeans.

141

Dad said, 'Good morning,' but Palermo didn't see him. He looked angry. We heard his voice coming over the speakers.

'What's that racket? Shut that off. Who's been singin' my song?'

The music stopped.

'We just did a vocal while we were waiting,' said the engineer's voice. 'I thought it would help the musicians to get into it.'

'Well don't think. Just do what I tell you. Nobody sings Murray's songs, except Murray. Get it?'

'Anything you say, Murray.'

'You're damm right it's anything I say. You let some no voice jerk sing my song again and you're out. Come on, let's get moving. I've got a plane to catch.'

Somebody switched off the microphone. I looked up at Dad. He was looking into his coffee. He drank it quietly but I knew he must have heard everything.

'He said it was his song,' I said. 'It's not his song.'

'Yes, but he doesn't know that yet.'

Dad walked back into the studio and I followed.

Murray Palermo had taken his jacket off. The photographer took a picture of him. There was a sudden flash of white light.

'What the Hell,' shouted Murray. 'What you doing?'

'Daily News,' said the photographer.

'I'm writing a story, sort of fly on the wall stuff about your recording session. Could we ask a few questions?'

Murray Palermo's face was suddenly covered in smiles. He shook them both warmly by the hand. 'Always glad to see you boys from the paper. Just make yourself at home, boys, make yourself at home while Murray cooks up a hit recording.' He walked into the studio and stood at the microphone. 'Let's go, boys,' he said. The photographer was creeping alongside him. When he saw him, Murray nodded in his direction and showed his teeth in a smile. He had a good strong voice. After a few bars though, he waved to the band to stop playing. There was silence. Everybody looked at him. During the silence Dad and I edged towards the engineer's booth.

'I can't sing this,' said Palermo. He threw the piece of paper with the song on it into the air. The small dark man ran forward and picked it up. He handed it back to Palermo. 'What is this with lift?' he shouted. 'I want these words changed. I can't sing this.'

He saw Dad for the first time. We were creeping as near to the wall as we could so as not to disturb anyone.

'Where the Hell have you been?'

'I've just been having a coffee, Murray.'

'You're not paid to drink coffee, Harry. You're paid to be here when I want you. Don't you drink your coffee in my time.'

I could see Dad's face going red. I knew he didn't want to upset anyone because he really wanted that song to be recorded properly.

Dad whispered to me, 'Go and sit in there with the engineer, Louie.' I started to walk away.

'Who's this?' demanded Murray staring at me.

'It's my son Louie. You met him in Southport, remember?'

Palermo began to stride around in anger.

'What the Hell is going on here? What the Hell is going on? I'm trying to cut a record here. This is important. It's serious and we have kids running round all over the place.'

'It's not kids, it's a kid. Just one, Murray.'

'Are you arguing with me? I never have kids in the recording studio. Never have and never will. Never! Never! Is that understood? Have you got that, Jerry?'

'Sure Murray,' said the little dark man.

I looked at Dad. 'D'you want me to wait outside?'

Dad put his hand on my shoulder. I could tell he was angry but his voice was calm, 'I asked you on Saturday if he could come. You said it would be O.K.'

'Saturday? That was last week. Am I supposed to remember things from last week?'

'He can sit with me,' said the engineer.

Dad pushed me towards the door and I went back to my seat on the sofa.

'All right, let's not waste more time.' He walked over to Dad. 'I wanted you here. Why weren't you here? I need some words changing. I . . . where's the words?'

'Here, Murray,' said Jerry running up to him and putting the piece of paper in his hands.

'I want this changed.'

'What's wrong with the words?' asked Dad.

'What's right with them is more the point. Where are we? They don't make any kind of sense to me.'

'Of course they make sense.'

Palermo looked Dad straight in the eye. 'Look, don't you argue with me boy. If I say it doesn't make sense, it doesn't make sense. Period.'

'What in particular, Murray?'

'You've got the word "drift" here. I want it changed.'

'Why do you want it changed? What's wrong with drift. I like drift.'

'Because I don't like it.'

'Why?'

'Because it doesn't rhyme. It doesn't rhyme with elevator.'

'It doesn't rhyme with elevator. It rhymes with lift.'

'It doesn't rhyme with elevator.'

'I haven't written elevator.'

'You'd better write it now then.'

'Why should I write it?'

'Because I tell you to, boy.'

'You tell me what's wrong with it and I'll change it,' said Dad walking after Murray.

Palermo turned round. 'Hear this everybody. You'll change it, first of all, because I say so; you'll change it, second of all, because this is an American song. We don't say "lift" in America. We say "elevator". Now change it.'

The reporter looked round. Lit a cigarette. 'Happy little fella, isn't he?' he said.

Dad came into the booth and asked for a pen. He was really angry. Murray came after him. Dad sat down by the engineer, looking at the paper.

'What rhymes with elevator?'

'You tell me,' said Palermo. 'For months you've been telling me what a great writer you are. Now you're asking me to do the writing. You're the writer. Write.'

Dad began moving his lips, tapping his forehead with the pen and staring at the ceiling. He was trying all the words that rhymed with elevator. Everybody else was doing the same. It looked as though we were all praying.

'Got it!' said Dad. Everybody looked at him.

'Alligator,' said Dad.

I thought Palermo was going to explode. 'Alligator!' he shouted. 'Alligator! This girl is going up in an elevator with an alligator! What is this? This is supposed to be a love song not a Horror Movie.'

'Her shoes are made of alligator skin,' explained Dad patiently.

Palermo snatched the paper from him. He mumbled through the words. 'It'll do,' he said.

'Let's go for it.' he said.

He went back in the studio and put the headphones on.

'I have a bit of a philosophy on recording, you guys from the press might be interested to hear. They call me One-Take-Murray. Now it's my belief if you ain't gonna get it right on one take you ain't never gonna get it right.'

'Can you hear yourself O.K.?' asked the engineer.

'I want more of me and give me some reverb.'

'I'd rather take it dry and add the reverb and effects after.'

Palermo took off his headphones and came into where we were sitting. 'What the Hell is going on here? Is this the way you do things? Let me tell you once, boy, and you listen real good. I want to hear me and I want reverb. Now! You got that.'

The engineer nodded.

'Good.' He went back into the studio.

He closed his eyes and started to sing again. About half way through Dad leaned over the desk and switched on the microphone so that he could speak to Palermo.

'Murray,' he said.

Palermo opened his eyes. The band slowed to a stop.

'Did somebody speak to me?'

'Murray,' said Dad, 'I don't think you're singing it how it's written.'

Palermo tore off his headphones. Everybody looked at the floor as he stormed in. All except Dad. He looked him straight in the eye.

146

'Yes?' he said. There were large rings of sweat under his armpits.

'Something wrong with my singing?'

'Murray,' said Dad calmly. 'The first verse is fine and the chorus but you're singing the second verse too hard. Too full out. Try laying back on it a little.'

There was a long pause.

'Let me ask you, Harry,' Palermo said speaking very quietly, 'how many records have you made?'

'All I'm saying, Murray, is when you get to that line in the second verse – And the moon is streaming through – that's a thoughtful kind of . . .'

'How many records?'

'I'm not telling you how to sing Murray. But this is my song. It's going to have my name on it and I want it sung how I intended it.'

'I'll tell you. None. Zero. Zilch boy. Now let me tell you something. All right. You listen good now. I have made forty-five albums. Twenty-five of which have made the Billboard Top Twenty. Ten of which have been in the top ten and three of which have made the number one spot. Now you have made, how many was it, did I hear No records? And you are telling *me* what to do with a song. This is Murray Palermo speaking, boy, and no small time no-hoper from way back, who I thought out of the kindness of my heart I could give a helping hand to, is going to tell me how to sing a song. Is that clear? IS THAT CLEAR? Right, let's try it again. And if I hear any more. I don't do the song.'

Palermo walked out and put on the headphones.

'Crazy Like the Moon, take four,' said the engineer.

The man in the waistcoat came through with a bundle of papers. He didn't know what was going on. He handed them to Dad. 'This is the agreement on the song. It's just a formality. If you'd like to sign both copies and keep one for your own records that'll be fine.' He looked round. 'Everything going well?'

'Oh fine,' said the reporter. He'd been writing everything down.

The man in the waistcoat turned to go.

'Hang on a second,' said Dad. He began to read the papers.

The band was counted in and Palermo launched into the song once more.

'It's all in order,' said the lawyer. 'It's our standard song writers' agreement.'

Dad carried on reading. Then he folded the papers and handed them back.

'Come on, Louie,' he said and stood up.

'Where are you going?' asked the lawyer.

'Where I should have gone months ago,' said Dad. 'Home.'

He opened the door into the studio. The band ground to a halt. Palermo opened his eyes in astonishment, as Dad and I walked past him. The lawyer followed him.

'What you mean by walking through the studio when I'm recording? Are you crazy?'

Dad turned round. 'Maybe I am. I'm sorry I can't let you do the song.'

Palermo's mouth dropped open. 'You can't . . .'

Dad looked at the floor and then at Palermo. 'I really wanted to put this song out. And, although it sounds strange, even though I think you're a grade one berk, I wanted you to sing it. It means a lot to me that song. More than I can say. It's a very good song. But it won't work.

148

According to this agreement you give me £150 for the song. In other words I get no royalty. I sell my claim on it, lock stock and barrel, to you.'

'That's right,' said the lawyer.

'The song stops being mine and becomes yours. For £150 I sell it to you like a pound of sausages. And when it goes on the streets, it'll have your name on it. Just like the other one. Only that time you didn't even pay me so I suppose that would be fairer described as stolen. I'm afraid I can't let you have the song.'

He turned for the door. 'Come on, Louie.'

Everybody looked at him in amazement.

'You can't walk out on me. Nobody walks out on Murray Palermo.'

'Watch me,' said Dad.

I thought Murray Palermo was going to explode. He came round in front of us. The veins were standing out on his neck. 'Let me tell you something, boy. Something you maybe don't know. You can't stop me. I can record that song whether you like it or not. And I can say it's mine whether you say so or not.'

'No you can't because it's my song.'

Palermo held up the sheet of paper.

'Who says so? It's our word against yours.'

'You say so.'

'I say so. You're crazy.'

'In front of those men from the paper. They heard you say that I wrote the song. You said it yourself. Isn't that right?'

The reporter and the photographer nodded.

'You . . .'

Palermo swung at Dad, who maybe was expecting it. He ducked. Palermo was off balance and Dad was able to

149

push him quite gently. He tumbled over backwards taking the drums and a microphone stand with him. Dad put his arm round my shoulder and walked me past the fountain. Suddenly I was hurled to one side. I ended up close to the fountain. Palermo and Dad faced one another. He was twice the size but Dad was strong and quick. They circled slowly, the lawyer tried to intervene. 'Gentlemen,' he said, but Palermo pushed him sprawling out of the way. Dad was facing me. Palermo had his back to me. He was backing towards me. I could almost touch his legs. Then I remembered something.

I caught Dad's eye. 'Dad, you've got the drop on him. You've got the drop on him now.' Dad stopped. Recognition and memory lit up his eye. He advanced slowly on Palermo. When he was a yard away, he dropped both his fists as if inviting a blow. Palermo drew back his fist to punch. As he did so, I grabbed his right leg with all my strength and sank my teeth into his calf. He gave a scream and half turned. At that moment Dad swung a punch from somewhere near his knees that caught him flush on the jaw. Palermo lifted off the ground and over my body. For a second he seemed to hang in mid-air. There was a vivid explosion of light as the flash gun went off and then he was flat out in the pool. The fountain played colourfully on his head.

'Let's go and see your Mum,' said Dad, pulling me to my feet. The band, the lawyer and the newspaper men looked on in silent amazement. At the door Dad turned back.

'Just a minute,' he said.

He walked past the staring faces and picked up the tape he'd made.

'Not for the record,' he said, 'just for me. It might remind me not to be such a fool.'

He walked out past the still figure of Palermo. He threw the contracts up in the air. They fluttered down and settled gently in the coloured water.

Chapter 13

We didn't get home till the next afternoon. Dad told me it was because there wasn't a train. But I had a feeling he was putting off facing my Mum. As usual he'd made up a big story about the song and how it would change their lives. That it was his last big chance. 'If the song does well,' he told her, 'I can stay at home and write my songs. I won't have to impress them; they'll be beating a path to my door.'

Dad should have been a salesman selling dreams. He could make you believe you could see things that just weren't there. I don't think Mum was taken in. She'd heard Dad's stories too often. She knew him inside out. It didn't really bother her. She just wanted Dad to be there whether he was a success or not. But she knew that big dreams and ambitions were as much part of Dad as the colour of his hair.

The nearer we got to our house the more nervous he became. Sometimes he'd talk non-stop and then he'd go quiet for about half an hour. He even started asking my advice. But he didn't give you a chance to answer the questions, he went right on and answered them himself. So he'd say, 'D'you think your mum'll mind? No, I don't think she'll mind. Will she? D'you think I should have told her about knocking Murray into the pond? Perhaps I should. She wouldn't understand would she? Yes she would.'

When we got to the front gate he couldn't get himself to go in. He kept lifting the latch and then closing it and walking up and down the street talking to himself. Then he'd come back and lift the latch and this time he'd get half way up the garden path then he'd be out in the road again, muttering, 'I shouldn't have come, I've let her down.' I was getting really bewildered watching him. For a time he sat on the wall opposite working out what to say.

'I'll go straight in and say, Kate, I'm back.' Then he shook his head. 'She'll know I'm back. She'll know. If I wasn't back I wouldn't be there to tell her.'

And he'd sit down again with his head in his hands. I was really getting fed up with opening gates and going in and coming out and sitting on walls and standing up and sitting down again.

Once he got as far as the front door. He was just lifting his hand to knock when he said, 'D'you think Edgar'll be there?'

When I told him there was no sign of his car he looked relieved but a couple of seconds later he was out in the street again saying, 'She doesn't want me. I know she dosn't want me.'

In the end he sent me to tell Mum that he was in the back garden. If she wanted to talk to him she could come out there. I felt like a messenger between two generals.

Mum hugged me and cried when she opened the door. She looked up and down the street. 'Where's your father?' she said.

When I told her, we both went to the back room and looked through the curtain. He was crouching down with Jo talking to her. His suitcase was in the middle of the lawn. Mum looked in the mirror and patted her hair. 'Fancy leaving his suitcase there,' she said.

I can't understand grown ups. They hadn't seen each other for about seven months and all my Mum could worry about was his suitcase being in the garden. I'd expected them to run towards each other and embrace.

'What's he doing out there?' she asked.

'He's not sure whether you want him back.'

'I don't think I do,' said Mum. 'I'm glad he's brought you back safe and sound but if he thinks I'm going to rush out there and fall on his neck and forgive him he's got another think coming. The idea. Why should I go out to him? I didn't run off like that. If he wants to see me, let him knock on the door and ask. Am I supposed to go out there and fall on my knees and beg forgiveness?'

Dad was galloping round the garden with Jo on his back. Mum went into the front room and sat down.

'Tell him he's to knock on the door and ask if he wants to see me. And that doesn't mean I'm taking him back.'

I went into the garden. Dad was walking up and down with his hands behind his back. 'What did she say?' he asked when he saw me.

'She says if you want to see her you've to knock and ask. Oh, and she said just because she's talking to you it doesn't mean she'll take you back.'

'Does she?' said Dad. 'Why doesn't she come out and tell me herself?'

'She says you're the one who's gone away. It's up to you.'

Dad started walking up and down again. He looked like Napoleon in that picture where he's just been captured.

'Tell her,' he said, 'tell her I know it was wrong of me to go off. I'm truly sorry and it won't happen again.'

Mum was at the kitchen door when I got to the house.

154

'I heard what he said,' she told me. 'Just tell him. I can't trust him. And a man I can't trust is no good to me.'

I ran back to Dad. He was closer by now.

'Can't trust me. I've given my word. I don't give my word lightly.'

'You gave it lightly every other time,' called my mother. She was in the garden by now.

'I did not.'

I called to Mum, 'He said he did . . .'

'I heard what he said,' she shouted. 'Just because you come back with those spaniel's eyes saying you're sorry, you think you'll break down my resistance. Well it doesn't work. You've let me down too many times. It's easy to say sorry you know. Anybody can say sorry. It's being here with me and the children, bringing home some money that's hard.'

'When have I ever broken my word? When? You tell me.'

I walked down towards the garden to where Jo was playing. They didn't seem to need me now.

'Every time. Every time you come home you say, "Never Again". But there never is a "Never again" for you. Never again only lasts as long as the next time it suits you to go wandering.'

'I meant it every time.'

'Meaning it and doing it are two different things.'

Jo was digging a deep hole. It was underneath some apple trees. She was banging one of Dad's spades into the ground. It was rusty, like all of Dad's things. I could imagine him going into a gardening shop and buying all these spades and forks and imagining this garden he'd have. But I never saw him working in the garden. Now the tools were rusty.

She put the spade down when she saw me. She jumped into the hole she'd made. It was over her knees.

'Where you going?' I asked her. 'Australia?'

'Where are my chocolates?' she said. 'You said you'd bring me chocolates.'

Dad and Mum were face to face now. Mrs Delaney next door had come to put her washing out. She'd really come to listen. They were still arguing.

'I had to go,' said Dad.

'I didn't mind you going when you were twenty or even thirty but when you're forty I expect a bit more sense.'

'I wasn't going for good.'

'How was I to know that?'

'It was you who wrote and told me not to come back.'

'Because I wanted to know where I was. At least if you didn't come back and it was definite, I'd know where I was.'

Jo was upset by all the shouting. She picked up the spade and ran round the garden shouting. 'Nonononono', over and over.

Mum said, 'Don't be childish, Jo.'

'I suppose you know where you are with Edgar.'

'Don't you say anything about Edgar. He's been very good to me.'

'That's what I heard.'

'What's that supposed to mean?'

I joined Jo in the hole. We both dug as hard as we could, not speaking. I remembered that story I'd read when I was about six. These two kids dig a huge hole and they come out in a big garden full of flowers and palm trees.

'I didn't mean anything about Edgar.'

'He's been very kind. I won't have him spoken of like that. At least he was here when he was needed.'

156

'Meaning I wasn't.'

'Meaning exactly that. Where were you when Jo was born and I had to sell the house? Or when Louie was two. You couldn't be there could you? You were off somewhere on the other side of the world, looking for Bob Dylan or something stupid. I've never felt safe. Never. I'd think for a month sometimes. This is it. He's got it out of his system and then I'd see this look come into your eyes and all I'd be left with was a wardrobe full of empty drawers and a letter on the mantelpiece saying how sorry you were.'

'But this was a good chance.'

'Did it work?'

'Well I . . .'

'Did it?'

'Not really.'

'What happened?'

'I decided not to do the song.'

'So that means you'll be off chasing other dreams.'

'No, I'm coming back.'

'And what am I supposed to live on? Dreams?'

'I'll get a job.'

'Who's going to give you a job? Edgar won't help you this time. Not after you walked out on the last one. Everybody knows you in this town.'

Dad pulled a roll of notes out of his pockets.

'That's what I saved, driving the bus.'

Mum turned away. 'Don't you understand? It's not money. I just want somebody solid. Somebody I know will be here next breakfast time. That's all. It's not asking for very much.'

'I would have sent you the money. I would have written. But you told me I wasn't to.'

He was really angry now and threw the roll of money

on the ground. I don't know what would have happened then. Maybe Dad would have stormed off for good. But just then a car drew up in the street and Uncle Edgar rang the front door bell. It was like in a boxing match where the two fighters have a rest between rounds. When nobody answered the door Uncle Edgar came through into the back garden. He couldn't see Dad or me and Jo from where he was standing by the garage. I could see Billy Fa Fa behind him by the gate. Jo and I ducked down into the hole and peeped over the edge. Uncle Edgar had a paper in his hand.

'Kate,' he said, 'I wonder if you've seen the latest disaster involving your wandering husband? It's just unbelievable.'

At that moment Dad took a couple of steps forward towards Uncle Edgar. I don't think he was going to do anything. Maybe he just wanted to talk to him. Uncle Edgar first saw the roll of notes on the ground. He frowned. Then he looked up and saw Dad for the first time. His face suddenly went pale. He made a sort of gargling sound in the back of his throat and started backing off as if he'd seen a ghost. He dropped the paper and turned and ran into his car and drove away as fast as he could. Jo and I looked at one another. We couldn't understand what had made him run off like that. I climbed out of the hole and walked over towards Mum and Dad. They were looking at each other in surprise. I was hoping Mum and Dad had calmed down. Jo was looking at the paper and pointing. Dad picked up the money and put it in Mum's hand.

'Daddy, Daddy,' said Jo.

'Not now, Jo,' said Mum.

But Jo insisted. She brought the paper over towards

where we were standing and pointed at something on the front page.

There was a large photograph of Dad in the act of punching. Murray Palermo's feet were off the ground. There was a smaller picture underneath showing Murray Palermo sitting in the pool.

Above the picture was written in large capitals:

'THIS WAS THE MOMENT WHEN POP TURNED TO BANG FOR THE SINGING COWBOY.'

Underneath was a long story that began:

'Punch Up In The Studio For Pop and Country Star.

Instead of being a *star* American hit-maker, Murray Palermo, was seeing *stars* when songwriter Harry (Hank) Langton (40) showed the chart topper what a hit really was. Harry, who has written Western adventure stories as well as starring in films with John Wayne, Burt Lancaster, James Stewart and other Hollywood all time greats, snapped when the big-head antics of the burly songster got too much to bear. The song is ended but the bruises linger on. Palermo left Britain with a closed eye yesterday afternoon. And he wasn't winking. "No comment" was his smart reply. As for Hank, he's gone to ground. And maybe that's the right place for someone who's better at handing out hidings than going into them. Come back soon Murray.'

We all looked at one another.

'Who told them about Western Adventure stories. I've never written stories,' said Dad.

Jo was jumping round the garden, punching the air.

'Daddy punch,' she kept saying.

I could see Mum wasn't at all pleased.

'And where did they get that business about me being a star?'

'I didn't say you were a star,' I said.

'Oh it was you, was it?' said Dad.

'I just said you'd acted with them. That was all.'

'That'll teach you not to talk to the newspapers. They'll twist everything you say.'

'So none of this happened?' said Mum. 'The papers made it all up I suppose.'

'Well no,' said Dad, 'some of it's true.'

'Who's going to give you a job now?' asked Mum. 'D'you think after seeing that all over the papers anybody's going to take you on?'

'Pow, zonk, crash,' shouted Jo, bouncing around the garden, laying waste to hundreds of imaginary enemies.

'Jo, stop that,' said Mum. 'You see how it's affecting the children?' she said, turning on Dad.

'They've got it all wrong. You've got it all wrong. I'm not a violent man. You know that. I didn't mean to hit him. I just went to talk to him, that was all,' said Dad.

'I see,' said Mum, 'so he got a huge bruise and fell into the pond because he likes doing that sort of thing.'

'I bit his leg,' I said. 'Then Dad hit him. I started it.'

'Oh that's wonderful. You've got your son at it now.'

'Pow! Splatt!' shouted Jo.

'We'll have a family of hooligans, then perhaps you'll be satisfied. Look at what happened with Edgar. He was frightened of being in the same garden with you.'

Dad went over to his suitcase and picked it up. 'Well,' he said, 'I'd better be off. It's obvious I'm not wanted here.'

He walked towards the gate.

160

Jo stopped playing and was quiet. I looked at Mum. Jo ran after him and then stopped. She looked back enquiringly at Mum.

'Mum, you can't let him go,' I pleaded. 'After all I've been through.'

Dad was opening the gate. He didn't look back.

'Harold,' said Mum. She took a couple of steps forward. Dad turned. 'You'd better come back.'

'Are you sure you want me to?' said Dad. 'I don't want pity.'

'It's not pity. The children need you.'

'What about you, Kate?' said Dad. 'Do you need me?'

'I don't know. You'll have to give me some time. I felt very bitter this time you know.'

Dad nodded. 'You won't know I'm here. You have your life, I'll have mine. Tomorrow I'll try and find a job. I mean it this time, Kate.'

'Yes well, maybe you do, Harold, but perhaps it would be best if you didn't make any promises. Then you won't disappoint me, will you?'

Jo had got hold of Dad's hand and was pulling him.

'I'll make you a bed up in the spare room,' said Mum. She was feeling better. That's how she was when she had something to do.

'No,' said Dad. 'You don't want me in the house. I know that. I'll, I'll . . .' He looked round. 'I'll be comfortable in that shed.'

'You can't sleep in the shed,' said Mum. 'What'll people think?'

But Dad insisted. Once the idea of the shed took hold there was no shifting him. Perhaps he wanted to be uncomfortable to pay for the things he'd done to Mum. It

161

was like a sort of punishment that made him feel better in a funny way.

Dad made the shed as comfortable as he could. He put up curtains and brought down a mattress. He wouldn't let anybody help him. When the mattress was in, there was hardly room for anything else. He brought out all his photographs and pictures. All those old film stars with their signatures scrawled across the bottom. On one wall was a map of America with all the places he'd been to. He had arrows leading from them and in a box at the side was the story of what happened there. He also pinned up his photographs of the Old West. Gunfighters and pictures of Tucson and Abilene and Wichita. He put up a wooden shelf on some bricks near the lawnmower and kept all his books about the American Civil War and the lives of cowboys on it. The shelf sloped a bit because Dad wasn't much of a handyman but it held the books up. It was as if Dad was making the shed into a treasure house of his past life. And he was really trying to get on with Mum. He was doing all sorts of jobs that he normally hated, like mowing the lawn and painting the windows. He was really trying to make it up to her. I think Mum could see this, but I think she'd been hurt too many times by Dad's disappearing tricks to be able to trust him. Every morning he looked through the paper for a job but there was nothing doing. He wrote scores of letters. Nobody replied.

As for me, I didn't feel too good about having a dad who lived in a garden shed. It's not something you want spread around, is it. When I went into town on the Thursday Mr Nelson got on the bus. I was hoping he wasn't going to see me. But he did. Mr Nelson is about twenty-three and teaches English. He has long black hair and a moustache. He combs his hair across at the top because he's going a bit bald, and wears lots of badges about C.N.D. and Save the Whales and being a Socialist Vegetarian. We're always doing projects with him. As soon as we finish on Transport Under The Sea we're on to something else. He's always getting you to sit by him and have little chats. He keeps telling you that he's like you really. That he understands what it is to be a kid under this government. Well, I didn't think that was true at all, because he was getting paid for a start. And he didn't have to be in school if he didn't want to. He's always calling you by your first name. And you're supposed to call him Geoff. But I used to call him Mr Nelson on purpose. All the time he's talking to you he nods his head as if you're saying something really serious. And he keeps saying, 'Right,' when you know that really you're talking rubbish. So he was the last person I wanted to sit next to.

He sat down slowly.

'Louie,' he said 'Louie.'

'Mr Nelson,' I said, as if I'd just noticed he was there.

'Right,' he said, and started nodding. Then straight away he was into asking questions. All about Dad and Mum not getting on.

He rolled one of these horrible smelling cigarettes.

'I know what it's like to be a kid and unhappy, believe me,' he said. 'There's these really difficult home situations that are really tough to deal with. Right?' He put his hand on my arm. 'I know what it's like to be a kid and unhappy, believe me. I know.' And up and down went his head. Without thinking my head started going up and down. With Mr Nelson the feeling I have is that I'm a bowl of stew and he's dipping his hands into me. I wondered if Billy Fa Fa'd been talking to him. Was he going to bring up the subject of the shed? Can you imagine how

163

embarrassing it is having a Dad who lives in the garden shed? Fancy walking round all day with that on your mind. Suppose the whole town knew?

'That's Louie Langton. His Dad lives in a shed.'

Suppose Sheila Whiteley had heard about it?

I kept smiling at Mr Nelson and telling him how everything was fine. In the end I pretended I'd seen someone I knew and got off the bus. He gave me a wave as the bus pulled past. I had to walk a mile into town but it was worth it to be rid of Mr Nelson.

The next morning there was a letter for me. I'd hardly ever had a letter before, except those long ones that Dad sent me that I kept in a box upstairs. Dad was having breakfast downstairs. It was as if he was getting back into the house a foot at a time. But Mum was keeping him at a distance. You could tell by one remark she made.

She said she'd promised to go to a concert with Uncle Edgar that night and she couldn't put it off just because Dad was home. Dad didn't say much. He knew he was on dangerous ground and was on his best behaviour. He just muttered under his breath something about Uncle Edgar being like a packet of cornflakes which is what he often called him. And Mum said, without looking up from the tea she was pouring, 'One thing about a packet of corn-flakes, it's always there at the breakfast table every morn-ing.' Dad didn't say anything after that. Just ate his breakfast quietly and went back to the shed. I went into the garden to open my letter. There were four white tickets inviting me to the Tennis Club Barn Dance. It didn't say anything on them. I didn't know if they were from Sheila Whiteley or not. Maybe Helen Darby had brought them round. Across them was written, 'To be paid for at the door.' In a backsloping handwriting. I looked at that handwriting for a long time. There was a ring at the front door and I heard Mum talking to someone. I took the envelope with me to the shed. I asked Dad if he would like to go to the Barn Dance on Saturday.

'Maybe your Mum would like to come,' said Dad.

We walked to the house. Mum was talking to a small round man with glasses. His eyes gleamed all the time. He had a brief case under one arm.

'Harold, this is Mr Rose,' said Mum. 'He's from Rose, Rose and Tyseley.' Mum raised her eyebrows.

'That's right,' said Mr Rose. 'Publishers you see. I read about you in the papers you see and well, I thought I'd pop round for a word. I wondered if you'd be interested in a proposition I have to make.'

Dad looked at Mum and raised his eyebrows.

'Strictly legal of course,' said Mr Rose, and laughed down his nose.

'Well,' said Dad. 'Why don't you come into my er . . . office?'

They walked out through the kitchen and into the garden.

'Office!' said Mum and gave a short laugh. She put the kettle on. 'Publishers,' said Mum. 'Wonder what he wants?'

I asked her if she wanted to go to the Barn Dance.

She said, 'Not really. You go with your Dad. I'll stay and look after Jo.' I thought it was a shame because Dad was trying so hard.

She seemed to know what I'd been thinking.

'You think I'm being hard don't you?' she said. 'I can't afford to be weak. You can get hurt just too many times. Your Dad's a good man at heart but he's always wondering what's round the next corner. His eyes look like

165

windows and you know before long he's going to be off again. He thinks the grass on the other side of the hill is always greener. But it isn't. It's the same grass but just a bit further away. The sad thing is that now I'll probably never be able to trust him. Here, take this coffee into the office.' She laughed when she said that.

When I came in with the coffee Mr Rose was sitting on Dad's mattress. His knees were right up in the air. Dad was sitting on the bar of the lawn mower. Mr Rose was looking round at Dad's maps and pictures.

'Ah,' he said, 'this is where you get your inspiration.'

'Inspiration?' said Dad.

'Perhaps I'd better explain myself,' said Mr Rose. He took off his spectacles and then immediatly put them back on again. 'You see, Hank — you don't object to my calling you Hank do you?'

Dad shook his head.

'You see, I run a publishing company and amongst other things, we do a Western magazine. It's about The Old West. It's informative, letters, pictures that sort of thing. There are a surprising number of people interested in that sort of thing. It doesn't have a large circulation, but it's growing. Everyone thought I was mad when I started it. We do a number of other magazines. But the West has always been an enthusiasm of mine. Don't know why. Must be in the blood. Anyway I thought you might be interested in writing for us, you see.'

'Writing?' said Dad. 'I can't write.'

'Modesty, modesty.'

'I've written songs. How did you — I mean what made you think I could write?'

'I saw the article in the paper. About the songs you'd written and the stories. Luke something or other. And then of course those Western films you acted in. Our readers would be very interested in those I'm sure.'

'But those films . . .' began Dad, but Mr Rose interrupted him with a wave of his hand.

'Very interested. We run a feature on old films once a month. Now that's the beginning. Now there's also a possibility of us expanding our market into books. Western novels. You'd be astonished how well they sell. It's not all Star Wars and Soap you know.'

'But . . .' said Dad.

'Now,' said Mr Rose, ignoring Dad's interruption, 'what I'm proposing is that you try a short story first. Send it to me. Let me have a look at it and if we like it, we'll publish it. I'll give you a small advance for that of course. Say, fifty pounds. Then we'll give you a retainer if we like what you do. After six months if things go well we'll ask for an outline of a novel and there'll be an advance against royalties for that too. We'll talk about the details later. For the moment I just want to see if you're in favour of the idea.'

There was a silence. Dad started to say something a few times. His mouth opened but then closed each time without saying anything.

'Why don't you think it over? Then give me a ring. Here's my card.'

At last Dad managed to say, 'But those Luke stories. I wrote those years ago. I don't even know where they are.'

He was walking Mr Rose back into the house.

'I know where they are Dad,' I said, before Mr Rose could say anything. I rushed up to my room. The box was under my bed. It was stuffed with pages and pages of letters going back nine or ten years. I rushed downstairs with them and put them all into Mr Rose's arms.

'Goodness me,' he said.

'Oh those old things,' said Dad, 'I didn't know you kept those.'

Mr Rose was looking through them. 'Fine,' he murmured, 'very interesting. Need tidying up of course and if you have a typewriter it helps but there's plenty of vigour here, plenty of imagination.'

He looked at Mum. 'Don't you think so, Mrs Langton?'

'Oh yes,' said Mum.

'Well let me hear from you as soon as you've got something for me.' He let himself out. 'Nice to meet you. Goodbye, goodbye.' He raised his hat and was gone.

Dad was stunned. He sat down on a chair in the hall and looked at us, his mouth open.

'I can't write,' he said. 'I haven't any paper.'

Mum went into the living room and came back with a loose leaf file full of paper. She dropped it on to Dad's lap. His mouth was still open.

'I haven't got a typewriter,' he said.

Mum disappeared once more. In a few moments she returned with an old typewriter.

'It's old, but it works. Any more excuses?'

'No, no,' said Dad and walked across the garden and into his shed.

We didn't see him for the rest of the day really. Mum got me to take him his dinner. He was just sitting staring at his map and the pictures. He looked at me then started eating his dinner.

I said, 'D'you want pudding? It's apple crumble.'

'I don't have to go anywhere. Nowhere no more. Just sit here and be out there at the same time you see.' He tapped his brain. He was like somebody shell-shocked. Half way through the afternoon he came into the house.

168

'How d'you spell wrangler?' he asked.

Mum gave him a dictionary and he went back to the shed. Now and then he came out and walked up and down amongst the apple trees at the bottom of the garden. He'd stop and stare up at the sky for ten minutes on end. His lips moved slowly. Then he went back to his shed again and we didn't see him again that day.

That night I was awoken by Jo shaking my shoulder.

'What's up?' I asked.

'Dunno,' she said. 'There's someone outside.'

'Outside where?'

'Garden,' she said.

I went with her back to her bedroom. There was a strange noise. I opened the window and peered out. There was a light on in Dad's shed. On the night air could be heard the insistent banging of a typewriter. I closed the window.

'It's all right,' I said. 'It's Dad.'

'Where is Dad?' she asked.

'Where?' I said. I tucked her into bed. 'He's a hundred years ago, out West.'

I went back to bed.

The next Saturday I went with Dad to the Barn Dance. He wore blue jeans and a green and black shirt. I couldn't see Sheila Whiteley anywhere. But Helen Darby asked me for two dances. There were bales of hay about the place and everybody was dressed as cowboys. I was only sorry Mum hadn't been there. You didn't really have to dance with one person because they were all these dances where you kept changing hands with everybody and shouting 'Yahoo' very loudly all the time. I was glad about that because I couldn't do old fashioned dancing.

169

Billy Fa Fa was there, but Uncle Edgar hadn't come. Maybe he was scared of being thumped into a pond by Dad. Dad seemed to know all the dances and shouted 'Yahoo' louder than anyone. He was really enjoying himself. Billy Fa Fa brought over some drinks for Helen Darby. He took the opportunity to say, 'Your Dad been in any more punch ups lately?' He said it really loud so everybody could hear.

I looked round the room really casually. 'No, actually,' I said, 'he's been too busy writing. Film stuff. Stories, novels you know that sort of thing.' I walked away saying, 'Excuse me there's someone I've got to talk to,' but I trod on his foot as hard as I could, accidentally on purpose. Just as I walked away I saw Mum coming in through the door dressed as a cowgirl. She had Jo with her. Jo had a holster on her hip and a small six shooter. She pulled it out and shot the vicar's wife. Then everybody else in sight. Dad came over, and Mum and he got up and danced together. I could tell he was pleased to see her.

Jo sat next to me with her legs swinging above the floor taking pot shots at the dancers. There was a ladies 'Excuse me.' Jo went off to dance with a spotty boy of nine. Mum and Dad looked really good together.

My cowboy boots were pinching me. I hated pointed boots. They were probably too small for me. I hadn't worn them for years.

There was a pair of shoes in front of me. I straightened up. Sheila Whiteley said, 'Are your feet good enough to dance?'

I felt the blush spreading up my neck and over the top of my head. She had a white blouse on. I put my hand on her back. I hoped it wasn't sweaty or dirty. I took it off and wiped it secretly on the back of my jeans.

'All right?' she asked.

'Fine,' I said.

I couldn't get over being this close to her. It was like when you have to sit up in the front row of a cinema at a film. It's all so close and too much for you. That's how it felt like dancing with Sheila Whiteley. I got this terrific feeling. I wanted to say her name to her. I'd never done that. I didn't want to say anything, just the name.

'Sheila.'

It nearly made me laugh me saying it like that. I couldn't help it. I said it again. 'Sheila.'

'Yes?'

I couldn't think of anything to say for a minute. I bet she thought this Old Time dancing was corny. I thought I'd better make it clear that I was into other kinds of music really.

'Not my sort of music this. I like the Stick Monkeys.'

She'd never heard of the Stick Monkeys.

'I quite like it,' she said. 'For a change.'

'Oh yes I like it all right,' I said.

'Did you get that bird out of the hedge?' she asked.

I couldn't think what she was talking about. And then I remembered. It seemed years ago. I decided to stop pretending. Look at the trouble it had got Dad into.

'Wasn't really a bird,' I said. 'I just got mad at somebody and punched the hedge. I didn't want to look stupid in front of you.'

She laughed at that. Really laughed a lot. I thought, 'It's good telling the truth. It makes girls laugh.'

She looked around the floor. I wasn't feeling tense at all now. I just kept putting my feet how she told me and counting 'One-Two-Three.' Mum and Dad were still dancing round together. Not doing any show-off dancing, just moving really smoothly.

Sheila nodded her head at them.

'Who's that?' she asked.

'That,' I said. 'Oh that's my mum and dad.'

The music stopped. Some people clapped. I hoped the music would start again soon so I could have another dance.

I thought about the train I'd travelled on and the ticket collector. Tony at the stables and being up in the aeroplane with Dad, looking down at all those houses.

'Where are you?' Sheila said.

'Where?'

'You were miles away,' she said, 'your eyes were . . .'

'Like windows?' I suggested.

She laughed and nodded. 'Something like that.'

The music started again. It was a fast one. I couldn't do it, but nothing was going to make me get off the floor.

We moved off together. 'I can't do this one,' I said. 'It's a fast one.'

'Come on,' she said. We whirled into the middle of the floor.

The music seemed to get louder.

Round we went. Dancing. Dancing.

Albeson and the Germans

JAN NEEDLE

It seems a very simple thing that starts off all the trouble – a rumour that two German children are coming to Church Street School. Although the teachers cannot understand the panic that this causes, Albeson can. His comics, and his dead grandfather have taught him all about Germans. And he doesn't fancy the idea one little bit.

The plan that Albeson's friend Pam comes up with frightens him stiff. Unfortunately, his mate Smithie, who's very tough and sometimes a bit odd, likes the idea. So Albeson has no choice. From then on, everything Albeson does gets him deeper and deeper into trouble, and finally, danger.

'Gripping, lively and funny – It really grabs you'

Daily Mirror

Daredevils or Scaredycats
Chris Powling

'Thanks for saving my place, Mush. I'll have it now.'

Fatty Rosewell was a big bully. Every Saturday he used threats and fists to get himself one of the best places in the cinema queue. When Fatty picked on David Clifford, he was looking his most weed-like, all glasses and hair, but weedy David gave all the kids in the queue, not least Fatty Rosewell, a big surprise that morning.

Sometimes it's hard to know where cowardice ends and bravery begins. The most unlikely scaredycats can suddenly turn into heroes. In the course of their adventures, Teddy, Kit, Pete and Jimmy begin to find out just how many different kinds of courage there are.

'Entertaining and realistic, the stories take us into a world of dare and counter-dare, bluff and counter-bluff, catcall and playground scuffle.'

Recent Children's Fiction

Private, Keep Out!
GWEN GRANT

I have written a book. It's all about the street we live on – me and our Mam and Dad, and our Pete and Tone, and Lucy, Rose and Joe. They're my brothers and sisters, worse luck.

I don't see why I should be nice to that stuck-up dancing teacher Miss Brown just because Pete's going to marry her, and how *can* you tell if angels are really men or women?

Growing up in a north-east Midlands colliery town just after the War, the narrator, youngest in a family of six, is never out of trouble. She is high-spirited, impulsive, stubborn and often exasperated by her parents and older brothers and sisters, but she will win the heart of every reader in her determined efforts to keep her end up.